They walked quic[...] path, as though b[...] way, they were se[...] of water spouting from the mouths of marble cherubs, gushing down waterfalls and swirling into lazy lagoons. It wasn't enough to calm her. This wasn't an aimless stroll. His pace was deliberate. Nick was searching for a place for them to hide together, rather than from each other. They stumbled across a coral-rock grotto with a narrow opening that let in a splash of moonlight. He pulled her inside.

She wiggled her hand free. "We could've talked outside."

He took a step, wandering deeper into the cave, marveling at it. "No, we couldn't."

"I don't know what you're thinking, Nick. I've changed."

"Are you sure? It's only been a year or so," he said, facing her now. "You look the same."

"I'm sure."

She stepped back and found there was no ground to gain; the cave was wide but shallow. Nick closed the gap between them.

The past echoed in the enclosed space. *Light of my life.*

"Nick."

His tone softened. "Come on, Leila. It's me."

Dear Reader,

Welcome to Miami, the city that is always hustling. Blame the heat, sticky humidity, clash of cultures or rise of the sea levels, but Miami is a city in a constant flux of renovation and expansion. Miami Dreams is a two-book series set in the world of high-end real estate. It features young professionals eager to secure a part of that multimillion-dollar business.

The women are smart, unquestionably ambitious and unapologetically sexy. Like the city itself, they have a Caribbean flair and hot tempers. When they meet the objects of their desire, their hearts combust.

The men are career driven and unstoppable until, of course, love brings them to their knees.

I hope you like it here as much as I do. Come to play, or stay and fall in love.

For notes on writing, illustrations and mood boards, follow me on Facebook at NadineGonzalezNovelist.

To lasting love!

Nadine

Exclusively *Yours*

Nadine Gonzalez

HARLEQUIN® KIMANI™ ROMANCE

Recycling programs
for this product may
not exist in your area.

ISBN-13: 978-1-335-21660-1

Exclusively Yours

Copyright © 2018 by Nadine Seide

All rights reserved. The reproduction, transmission or utilization of this work in whole or in part in any form by any electronic, mechanical or other means, now known or hereinafter invented, including xerography, photocopying and recording, or in any information storage or retrieval system, is forbidden without written permission. For permission please contact Harlequin Kimani, 22 Adelaide St. West, 40th Floor, Toronto, Ontario M5H 4E3, Canada.

This is a work of fiction. Names, characters, places and incidents are either the product of the author's imagination or are used fictitiously, and any resemblance to actual persons, living or dead, business establishments, events or locales is entirely coincidental.

® and TM are trademarks of Harlequin Enterprises Limited or its corporate affiliates. Trademarks indicated with ® are registered in the United States Patent and Trademark Office, the Canadian Intellectual Property Office and in other countries.

For questions and comments about the quality of this book please contact us at CustomerService@Harlequin.com.

H HARLEQUIN®
™ www.Harlequin.com

Printed in U.S.A.

Nadine Gonzalez was born in New York City, the daughter of Haitian immigrants. As a child, she was convinced that NYC was the center of the universe. But life has its twists and turns, and eventually she landed in Miami. She fell in love with the people, the weather and the unique mix of cultures. Now this vibrant city has become her home and muse.

Raised on a steady diet of soap operas, Harlequin romances, music, movies and classic literature, Nadine hopes to infuse her novels with her diverse influences.

A firm believer in work-life balance, Nadine is a lawyer, but also a fashionista, political junkie, art lover, amateur illustrator, wife and mother. You can reach out to her on Facebook, Instagram and Twitter.

Books by Nadine Gonzalez

Harlequin Kimani Romance

Exclusively Yours

For Ariel and Nathaniel, my loves. You make my life beautiful.

Acknowledgments

For my parents, who have always encouraged me to work hard and strive for excellence.

For Ariel, who made this dream come true.

Thank you, Dominique, Murielle and Martine, my siblings, for all the laughs. You make life fun. Warm thanks to Martine, best little sister and most loyal friend anyone could have. And thanks to my cousin Pascale and my dear friend Sarah for believing in me from the start.

Thanks to the vibrant local writing community and the amazing writers I've met at the Miami Book Fair workshops: Roxanna Elden, Natalia Sylvester, Terrence Cantarella and A. J. Hug, who have helped shape the early drafts of the "real estate" manuscript. #MiamiWrites

Finally, I am grateful to the editors at Kimani Romance—Shannon Criss, for her expert guidance, and Keyla Hernandez, for discovering, nurturing and championing my work.

Prologue

Leila was ready for a night at home, fuzzy socks and Chardonnay, when a friend called with an irresistible offer. "I can get you into the Vizcaya event. Raul Reyes is hosting. Interested?"

Reyes was a local real estate mogul. He owned everything. In Leila's line of work, he was king. Getting on the list was a coup, even for her friend Sofia, an event planner with seemingly endless contacts. Still, Leila hesitated. "I don't know. Are you going?"

"Can't," Sofia said. "But I'm pretty sure you can."

"And what? Go by myself?"

"*Sí, amiguita.* You're old enough. Put your big-girl panties on and go network like a boss."

Leila sat on the edge of her bed. She fought the urge to crawl under her sheets.

Sofia was relentless. "Do I have to remind you how terrible your last quarter was?"

"No, you don't."

Since opening her agency nine months ago, Leila was stuck in the low-rent market, helping college grads find one-bedroom condos and getting newlyweds into starter homes. After a dismal holiday season, during which she'd had to take a cash advance from her AmEx card to give her one employee a bonus, she was at the end of her rope.

"You should be thanking me. What else do you have going on this weekend?"

"What weekend? It's Thursday."

"It's Miami. The weekend started eight hours ago."

Later, as she stepped from the shower, Leila strategized. She'd get in, canvas the place with business cards and get out. Hit and run. She brushed her coffee-colored hair and swept on lipstick with a sure hand. Her bedroom window let in very little sunlight, but tonight it framed a perfect full moon, the first of the new year. It called for more daring. She stood naked in front of her open closet and wondered when she, a third-runner-up Miss Naples USA, had become the girl who'd rather stay home with cheap wine than go to a party alone. *I mean, come on!*

She reached past her collection of standard little black dresses for a red lace dress so delicate it bordered on lingerie. It was tucked into the back of her closet, part of a forgotten wardrobe from a time when she'd dressed to look sexy instead of smart—a habit that had only landed her in trouble. Funny enough, the red dress was one of the most conservative of the lot. It was time to get her mojo back. Time to get noticed.

Things were well under way by the time Leila made it to Vizcaya. She entered the villa through an arched doorway and fell in awe. Despite living her entire life in Florida, this was her first visit to the private residence turned museum. She'd expected tasteful elegance, not this riot of gold leaf, tile and mosaics. But she loved it and suspected Marie Antoinette would've felt right at home.

She ventured out to the grand terrace and camped near a cigar-rolling station. A band was setting up. The guests came together, mingled and broke apart in a well-choreographed dance. Waiters in fedoras and white *guayaberas* paid homage with their uniforms to Cuba, Reyes's birth country. And, surprise! All the extravagance was to celebrate the publication of the mogul's first book, *A New City: 7 Strategies for Urban Development.* The cover featured a photo of Reyes dating back to when he'd had a full head of black hair. Copies were piled on bar height tables everywhere. Some served as makeshift coasters.

Leila spied a white-haired Reyes holding court in a remote corner, his young, pretty, third wife at his side. She knew better than try to approach him.

A familiar-looking brunette peeled away from his entourage. Leila looked to the sky, trying to remember. Paige… Paige Conner. They'd met at a charity fundraiser Sofia had forced her to attend. Was Paige in marketing or accounting? It didn't matter. The king was inaccessible. A royal subject would have to do.

Moving quickly, she caught up with the brunette at the bar. Paige was chatting with a bartender with dimpled cheeks. Leila approached and, from a limited selection of red and white wines, ordered a glass of Sauvignon Blanc. Then, relying on her even more limited acting skills, she turned to Paige and cried, "Don't I know you?"

Paige looked up, blinking in confusion. "Sure," she said hesitantly, "we met at that thing, right?"

She appeared to be playing along out of courtesy or pity. Leila swallowed her pride and pushed forward. "Yes, that fundraiser thing."

The bartender served their drinks. Paige had picked red. Raising her glass, she dismissed Leila with a polite smile. "Good seeing you!"

Leila scrambled to keep the conversation going. "I'm just glad to see a familiar face. I don't know anyone here."

Paige took a healthy sip of wine and asked, "But you're having fun, right?"

"I'm not here for fun." With no time to waste, she got straight to the point. "I was hoping to meet Reyes. I'm dying to work with him. The man is a visionary! He practically created the Design District. And that new building downtown…wow!"

Paige squinted. "What do you do again?"

"Wait one second." She pretended to search her tiny purse for a business card and feigned relief to have found one. "Here you go."

"'Leila Amis,'" Paige read. "'Licensed real estate broker.'"

"That's me!" She sounded like an idiot.

"Okay. I know the deal," Paige said wearily. "You want me to pass this along?"

"That would be great."

"I'll try to get this into the right hands, but the sales team has a rock-solid lineup, so…"

"I get it," Leila said. "And, thanks."

Paige dismissed her with a wave of the hand, turning her attention back to the bartender. Leila happily melted into the crowd and headed for the villa.

One down. One hundred to go…

A waiter approached with a tray of mojitos, each cocktail glass stuffed with mint leaves and garnished with a sugarcane stick. Leila gladly exchanged her traditional wine for the more exotic drink. Spanning the elegant loggia, she caught her reflection in a massive gold-framed mirror. She looked good, her brown skin shimmering in the light of the chandeliers, her eyes brilliant with excitement. What a confident party crasher! She looked like she was actually having fun. Using the mirror to spy on the crowd, she sipped her cocktail and searched for her next target.

That's when she thought she saw him.

No big deal. He'd appear in crowds, only to vanish at closer inspection. Leila was used to it. He still lived in the ruin he'd made of her heart.

She glanced over her shoulder and the usually fleeting impression held. That chiseled face softened by a wave of brown hair… Who else could it be?

Standing only feet away and flanked by two admiring women, he towered over a small group. Leila's reaction was physical. A cramp in her gut. When she spun around, the confident woman in the mirror was gone, replaced with someone new but sadly familiar. Her instincts told her to run.

She took off, slicing through the crowd on her way out to the terrace. The band started up, playing a languid bolero. Couples came together under the full January moon—a moon that now appeared to be mocking her.

What's he doing in Miami?

The answer was irrelevant; she'd always known this day would come. But when she'd dreamed up scenarios in which they ran into each other—an airport terminal waiting to board international flights, a fabulous party very much like this one—she'd always managed to keep her cool. And now she looked around, disoriented, damn near hyperventilating. She'd reached the edge of the terrace. A vast, formal garden stretched out before her, drenched in darkness.

Taking a minute to weigh her options, Leila noticed something stuck to the sole of her stiletto. She checked. It was her business card stained red with wine.

Really?

It had been a mistake to come here. She had to get out. Fast. Maybe he hadn't seen her? Maybe she could sneak out?

"I remember that dress."

The long rope of "maybes" swung uselessly in the air around her.

"Please, I don't want a scene."

"Then you shouldn't have worn that dress."

Arrogant as always! She swiveled to confront him, waving her empty cocktail glass. "What are you even doing here?"

Nicolas Adrian. Once one of Miami's top brokers, he'd forfeited the title when he'd moved to Manhattan. That should've been the end of him.

He took the glass from her and set it on a nearby stack of books. "I'm here. No reason."

Leila felt betrayed. All those expensive, guided meditation classes she'd taken had been for nothing. The universe should have sent her a warning.

He extended a hand. "Come with me."

"I'm not going anywhere with you."

"We can have it out right here, if you like?" His tone was unyielding. She had a glimpse of the man she knew well, the tough negotiator. "I don't care who hears us, but I bet you do."

She gave up the fight. It was that easy. "You get five minutes." Taking his hand felt as natural as slipping on the dress.

Nick guided her down the stone stairs leading to the garden, which turned out to be a world unto itself. They walked quickly along the hedge-lined path, as though being chased.

Along the way, they were serenaded by the sound of water spouting from the mouths of marble cherubs, gushing down waterfalls and swirling into lazy lagoons. It wasn't enough to calm her. This wasn't an aimless stroll. His pace was deliberate. Nick was searching for a place for them to hide together rather than from each other. They stumbled across a coral rock grotto with a narrow opening that let in a splash of moonlight. He pulled her inside.

She wiggled her hand free. "We could've talked outside."

He took a step, wandering deeper into the cave, marveling at it. "No, we couldn't."

"I don't know what you're thinking, Nick. I've changed."

"Are you sure? It's only been a year or so," he said, facing her now. "You look the same."

"I'm sure."

She stepped back and found there was no ground to gain; the cave was wide but shallow.

Nick closed the gap between them.

The past echoed in the enclosed space. *Light of my life.*

"Nick."

His tone softened. "Come on, Leila. It's me."

Oh God, yes. She closed her eyes, all her late-night fears confirmed. He had only to say her name and her resolve turned into confectioner's sugar.

Nick moved closer and threaded a hand through the high slit of her dress, brushed her thigh.

He had no right to touch her that way. Why wasn't she fighting it?

The truth rose around Leila like floodwater. Her posturing was a ruse. All along she'd been actively plotting her capture. A fish seeking the fisherman's net. He was the man who'd once called her his prize. And tonight, despite everything, she wanted him to win.

Leila drew him to her and kissed him full on the mouth. He tasted like mint and sweet cane.

Nick came alive. He pressed her into the cave wall and ran his palms over her body, rediscovering familiar terrain.

She'd expected him to take her by storm, to invade her. But his touch was unhurried, deliberately slow. He knew he had her.

The scent of wild orchids and damp earth enveloped them. She was water, the bay at high tide. He was rock, the one obstacle she could not overcome. He gathered the soft lace of her skirt. She eagerly unfastened his belt. He grabbed her hands and whispered in her ear, "Tell me what's changed."

Leila had no answer. She let him take her, the rough surface of the wall biting into her back. Over the distant party music she heard him groan, heard him murmur her name over and over until her moaning took over, filling the cave.

PART ONE

Chapter 1

Leila had not—*not at all*—set out to be the girl who sat at her desk pining for the guy in the office with a view. She had big plans and her own reasons for taking the job at Kane & Madison Realty. But that's exactly the girl she'd turned out to be. The transformation happened on a bright summer morning, a year and a half ago, on her very first day on the job.

To shake off the jitters, Leila slipped out of her North Miami apartment at dawn for a quick run. Keys and pepper spray in hand, she sprinted along upper Biscayne Boulevard. She was hounded by a feeling that her tightly sealed world was about to crack open. It didn't make sense—a job was a job was a job, after all. If it didn't work out, she could always go back to retail.

She made it home, out of breath and still very anxious. The small apartment was quiet, her roommate asleep. After a quick shower, she studied her reflection in the steamy mirror a long while. She hadn't slept well and it showed. She swept on concealer then bronzer to liven her matte brown complexion. Much better. Her pageant days were behind her, but the tricks of the trade were hers for life.

Then, on impulse, she did the thing she rarely ever did except under exceptional circumstances. She pulled a wooden box out from under her bed. Inside, among several keepsake items, was a sparkly but flimsy tiara. She placed it on her head and studied her reflection again. She was ten, a little girl playing dress-up. A skinny, awkward child, she'd longed for grace, poise and a smile that could bankroll her dreams of escape. All she'd ever wanted was to escape her sleepy hometown in the outskirts of Naples, Florida, and create a new life, a big life, somewhere exciting. Over a decade later, she still wanted those same things.

You can do this.

She placed the tiara in the box and the box under the bed.

In the kitchen, Leila filled a travel mug with coffee and skipped breakfast. She was as antsy as a child on the first day of school and, in her pleated skirt and Mary Jane pumps, very much dressed like one. She'd never had an office job and her wardrobe proved it. *I'm out of my element.* No! *I'm finding my way.* She glanced at the oven clock. *And I'm wasting time.*

From the outside, the Brickell Avenue high-rise was sleek and modern. Inside it was sterile with marble floors, leather seating and paintings of palm trees bending to hurricane-force winds. Or was this true of all office buildings? Up until a week ago, she'd worked at Bal Harbour Shops. When she thought of the designer boutiques, koi ponds and actual palms trees, this place fell short. But if she wanted a fresh start, this was where she needed to be.

Leila followed the manager past a row of offices, hiding her disappointment with a careful smile. Jo-Ann Wallace wasn't fooled by her performance. The sharply dressed woman pointed to an open cubicle fitted with a steel desk and ergonomic chair. A window offered a view of a parking lot spread wide like an asphalt lake. "This is yours."

"Oh, nice! A window."

"The better views are for the top associates. Speaking of which, we hired you to work with one of our best. He comes to us from headquarters in New York and travels there often. Part of your job will be to keep him up to speed when he's away. Come. I'll introduce you."

Jo-Ann took the lead, head high, so proud of her position of gatekeeper to the throne. Leila fell one step behind. Maybe this was a mistake. Maybe she was wrong for this job. Was it too soon to quit? Was it quitting if you hadn't worked a day? *Oh, enough!* She willed herself to snap out of it, whatever "it" was. At an age when most girls stayed home battling acne, she'd stared down panels of judges wearing nothing but a bikini and a pair of heels. To now be intimidated by these office drones? Ridiculous.

The nameplate on the door adjacent to her workspace read *Nicolas Adrian, Associate*. Determined to make a good first impression, she smoothed her hair and squared her shoulders.

Jo-Ann raised her hand to knock, but stopped at the sound of laughter on the other side of the closed door. Mr. Adrian was apparently having a good old time, engaged in a lively telephone conversation that might or might not be work-related. He followed statements like "I had a great time last night" with "Is that really your best offer? Can't you come higher?" Leila focused on the voice. Low in tone, smooth and without the hard snobbish edge she'd grown accustomed to with the patrons of Bal Harbour Shops. It immediately roped her in.

"He sounds nice," she said.

Jo-Ann frowned. "The associates are sharks. There's nothing 'nice' about them. Don't say I didn't warn you."

There was nothing "nice" about Jo-Ann, either.

The door swung open. Both she and Jo-Ann jumped back, confronted by a pair of inquisitive inky-blue eyes. Nicolas Adrian filled the doorway. He wore a beautifully tailored navy suit with a starched white shirt open at the collar. His golden complexion betrayed a devotion to the sun. If he was a shark, Leila thought, he was a Great White.

"Good morning. How can I help?"

Jo-Ann stretched her neck to confront him. "Nick, meet your new assistant, Leila Amis."

Ignoring Leila, he asked, "What happened to Monica?"

"You *know* what happened to Monica."

"I really don't."

Jo-Ann maintained a firm silence during which Leila

tried to connect the dots. Had Jo-Ann switched out his assistant without him knowing? Did she think he wouldn't notice? His frustration with the woman was clear. Leila wanted to grab him by the shoulders and force him to acknowledge her. But when he did turn his gaze to her, she wasn't prepared, and very nearly stumbled backward.

"I'm sorry," he said. "I don't mean to be rude."

Maybe this was her way out. "If there's a problem, I can go."

"No!" the two cried in unison, finally agreeing on something.

"There's no problem. It's all sorted out," Jo-Ann said. "You wouldn't be here if it wasn't."

"Leila, it's nothing personal," he said. "I'm sure we'll get along."

He said her name as if he'd always known her. And she knew his type. Nicolas Adrian was a flirt—a gorgeous, blue-eyed flirt.

"Go ahead and get settled," Jo-Ann said. "You'll be in training most of the day."

Leila scurried off to her desk, adjusted the seat and found a cubby for her purse. The top drawer was stocked with office supplies. She grabbed a pen and a pad with the agency's uninspiring logo: a Welcome Home mat.

Note to self, she wrote. *That man is trouble.*

After that initial five-minute meeting, she didn't see much of her new boss. Jo-Ann had her shadow a few other assistants for quick one-on-one training sessions. That whirlwind desk tour gave her insights into the office dynamics. Jo-Ann was treacherous. Emilia, the receptionist, was a gossip... Nick, Tony and Greg were the youngest and coolest associates—the Big Three... A female associate? She quit... Greg gave the best holiday gifts... Tony was cheap, but worked hard.

"What about Mr. Adrian?" Leila worked up the courage to ask during the two o'clock coffee break. While one woman stirred a small amount of espresso into a whole lot of sugar, they all responded. The opinion was mixed, ranging from high praise to the down and dirty.

"You mean Nick? He can do no wrong in my book. He's a saint. Saint Nicolas!"

"He's no saint, and I'm willing to prove it. All I need is five minutes alone with that man. Make it ten."

Still others had an ax to grind. "How would I know? Monica kept him all to herself."

Late in the afternoon, she was at the reception desk learning the complexities of the telephone system—"…and to transfer calls press 7"—when her earlier fears returned. Would her plan work? Was she staring down a future based on how aptly she could transfer a call?

Then he showed up. For all his lauded virtues, he looked like the devil in a bespoke suit. *Saint Nicolas, my ass!* There was something about him that magically erased her emotional browser history. Ex-boyfriends, old crushes, broken hearts: delete. There was just him standing there, looking squarely at her.

Emilia, true to her reputation, was hanging on his every word. Not that he said much.

"Leila?"

"Yes."

"I'm heading out. See you in the morning."

"Good night, Mr. Adrian."

A pause. "Okay. Don't call me that."

And then he was gone, out the double-glass doors heading toward the elevators. Emilia tugged on Leila's sleeve. "Girl, you lucked out."

On the drive home, Leila didn't feel so lucky. Had she won the lottery of bosses or inherited a colossal clusterfuck? What was the deal with Monica, anyway? No one would say. Nicolas Adrian couldn't be any more attractive. Just thinking about him made her hot. So much so, she switched off the struggling AC and rolled down the windows of her Mazda roadster for much needed fresh air.

As she pulled into her building's parking lot, Leila caught sight of her roommate, Alicia. A few months ago, Leila had confidently responded to her Craigslist ad, figuring a female college student was a safe bet. She hadn't been wrong. Working on a graduate degree in social work at Barry University, Alicia spent most of her time there. Leila knew she was heading to class now and wouldn't be back until late.

"Hey," Alicia said. "How was your first day on the job? Learn anything?"

Leila stepped out of the car. "I learned how to transfer calls. I'm an ace at it."

Alicia snickered.

A firm believer that women in general, and women of color in particular, should stay in school and earn every degree possible, she'd practically begged Leila to go back to college. "You're too smart," she'd said. "There are dumber people than you working on PhDs." But Leila had been convinced that she'd strayed off the conventional path and was too far along to find her way back. Besides, she owed it to herself to follow her instincts.

"And how's the boss? The typical jerk?"

"Oh, no," she said without thinking. "He's butter on toast."

Alicia shifted under the weight of her backpack. "High in carbs and trans fat?"

They shared a laugh before Leila said, "Warm and delicious."

"Yeah," Alicia said. "But really, really bad for you at the end of the day."

We'll see, Leila thought, skipping up the stairs leading to their third-floor apartment.

A half hour later she woke from a dream where Don't Call Me Mr. Adrian had her naked on his desk and she was purring, "All I need is ten minutes."

Heart racing and covered in sweat, she sat up on the couch where she'd dozed off fully dressed. She brushed her hair out of her face and absently unbuttoned her blouse, tossing it on the carpet floor. *Am I going to be able to work with this man?*

The answer came swiftly. *You can and you will.*

Really, what choice did she have? If she quit one more thing, she'd officially be crowned Ms. Quitsville USA.

Chapter 2

That evening Nick met with Monica for dinner. Losing her had been a blow—a blow from which he'd fully recovered once Leila had shown up. Had he gained something better? That question left stones of guilt in his gut and kept him from relaxing in Monica's company.

They'd chosen a sushi restaurant close to the office. Monica had put some care in her appearance. Her red hair was styled in crafty spiral curls. She was proud and wouldn't want him to feel sorry for her.

"Listen," he said, cutting through the small talk. "I made a few calls. I might've found you something."

He placed a business card on the empty square plate before her. She snatched it up. "A nonprofit?"

"I know, it's not—"

"No. It's great."

"Lower pay."

"Better hours, typically."

"Okay, then." Since having her twins, time was more valuable than currency. "Give them a call. They're expecting you."

"Thanks, Nick," she said. "I'm going to miss you."

Her green eyes were glassy with tears. Feeling unsettled, he asked, "Sake or beer?"

"You know me. Beer."

When their waiter came around, Nick placed their orders, happy for the distraction. Then she asked, "Are you going to miss me?"

"How can you ask me that?"

For all intents and purposes, Monica had been his partner in crime. And it bothered him that, consciously or not, he'd shelved her in the past.

The waiter returned with their beers and a wooden bowl

of edamame. Monica reached for a pod and sucked on it, murmuring something about sea salt. He sipped from the bottle as a new silence settled between them.

"I heard the new girl started today."

He nodded. "I gave Jo-Ann hell."

"I heard she's pretty enough."

"Who are you talking to?"

"Just answer the question."

"You didn't ask one."

The waiter returned with Miso soup as Monica glared at Nick from across the table. "I'll admit it. I don't like to be replaced. And to hear that you're gushing—"

"Come on, Money…"

The pet name worked like magic. She relaxed and dropped the subject.

"I've got to get back to work." She picked up the large soup spoon. "Daytime TV is the worst. One court show after another. I didn't pull the kids out of day care, you know. I figured—"

Nick ignored his soup. He couldn't drop it. "Who said anything about gushing? I'm being nice. She's a sweet girl."

Monica looked confused for a while and then dropped her spoon and exploded. "Oh crap, you're crushing on her!"

Now he knew she really needed to get back to work. She was making this into a soap opera. "I don't know what they told you—"

"I can't say too much without revealing my sources."

He already knew her sources. "Don't bother. It's all bull."

"I don't work for you anymore, so I'm going to go ahead and be honest."

"When have you ever held back?"

"You'd be surprised."

He laughed. "What's your take? You think I fell in love in a day or something?"

Monica's gaze narrowed on his face. "Who's talking about love?"

She had him there. "No one."

"But you think she's beautiful."

Nick didn't *think* it. It was a fact. His thoughts ran to the moment he'd opened his door and found her there, packaged like a gift in that flirty skirt and heels. Arguably, it was an odd choice for a first day on the job, but he'd loved it. Those legs, that skin… He wished they'd met under different circumstances. He'd have enjoyed getting her out of those silly clothes.

Monica cleared her throat. She was still waiting for an answer.

"I think she's gorgeous."

Monica shot up, raising her fist in victory. "I knew it!"

Nick tapped his foot against the metal leg of the table, waiting for her to settle down.

She took a sip of beer and composed herself.

"Monica, it doesn't mean anything."

"Want to know what I think?"

He looked at her, unguarded, waiting.

"I knew you'd fall hard for someone someday. You're not the player you think you are."

"That day is not today, babe."

"I hope so," she said. "Chasing some girl around a desk is not your style. Plus, you need more than an office wife."

"You mean a second office wife. My first wife walked out on me and married a nice guy."

"I was fired. Don't rewrite history."

"More romantic my way."

"Promise you won't do anything stupid."

"I worked with you and you're the sexiest thing around."

"I wasn't fishing for a compliment, but thanks. I needed to hear that," she said. "Still. I think you should be careful."

"What do you think's going to happen?" He asked because he really wanted to know. How was this going to play out? Leila would be there tomorrow and the next day. And he wasn't about to change. His sexual life had never been about self-denial.

"Nothing will happen to you," Monica said gravely. "But Jo-Ann will drum that girl out of K & M so fast she won't know what hit her."

Chapter 3

Sharks move constantly, Leila observed her second day on the job. Nicolas Adrian arrived late and left early, wheeling a black, hard-shell suitcase behind him. "I'll be in New York the rest of the week. See you Monday." Leila was relieved. It gave her a full week to get settled and to focus on her training. But then he returned sooner than expected. Early Thursday, she heard him down the hall, swapping stories with Tony and Greg.

Simply hearing his voice caused Leila's pulse to skip. She told herself it was natural to be nervous, her hands trembling as she tidied her desk. She dumped a half-empty cup of yogurt. Beside her keyboard was a framed photo of her in full pageant regalia posing next to her aunt Camille, a Diana Ross lookalike. A stranger might mistake them for mother and daughter based on their similar broad smiles alone. Leila grabbed it and tucked it in a bottom drawer.

When he finally rounded the corner, followed by the other two, her desk was tidy but her emotions were a mess. Her eyes rushed to his face. Nicolas Adrian was a striking man. The hard lines of his face could turn off the romantics and the dreamers, but those blue eyes certainly could turn them back on.

"Hey there, Leila."

"Mr. Adrian. Good morning. You're back early." Her voice was weak, betraying her.

He rested a cup of Starbucks coffee on her desk. "For you. I don't know how you like it, so I improvised."

She reached for the cup. "It's fine. Thanks."

"Just tell me what you like. For next time."

"Milk. Sugar."

"A latte, then."

To save money Leila had avoided Starbucks, brewing

coffee at home. Miami's party scene was pricey. She spent enough on cocktails every weekend and didn't need an expensive coffee habit, too. If a latte equaled coffee plus Coffee-mate, she'd be fine.

"I'm not picky, Mr. Adrian. Whatever works."

"Stop calling me that."

Damn it. She needed the buffer that formality provided. She needed that shield. This was his second warning, though, and she'd have to stop. "Okay. What do I call you?"

"You know my name."

Her grip tightened around the paper cup and the heat seared her fingertips. The group moved into his office. Before the door closed behind them, she heard Tony say, "Your new girl is hot."

Nick's quick response was cutting. "Back off."

She didn't see much of him after that. He'd left for lunch at noon, called in a few times, but never returned, which was fine because she had to recover from that brief morning exchange. The next day, Friday, he made an appearance around three. Instead of saying, "Good afternoon. How are you getting along? Do you have any questions?" He gestured for her to follow him. "We've got a new listing."

She grabbed a pad and pen and trailed after him. This marked her first time in his office. The walls were bare except for matted and framed bachelor's and master's degrees in business administration; the first from University of Toronto, the second from NYU. Leila thought of Alicia—"Get a degree! Any degree!"—and felt sick. She focused on a bank of windows showcasing the chaotic mess on Brickell Avenue. The gridlocked traffic looked like a parade of luxury cars.

Nick handed her a sticky note with an address scribbled on it. "I want this property photographed right away. Call Chris Hopper. His number is in the master file. Tell him to meet me there around four, if he can."

"And if he can't?"

"Call that other guy. No, call Suzanne. She does good work."

Leila returned to her desk and frantically scrolled through the master file, an elaborate spreadsheet of Monica's creation. Chris Hopper agreed to the appointment. Nick was on his phone when she popped in to tell him. He mouthed, "Great." Soon thereafter, he came out with keys in hand.

"Ready?"

"Ready for what?"

"A site visit." He glanced at his watch, a sleek Patek Philippe with a black-lacquered face. "Or is it too late? I never asked. Do you have kids? Monica couldn't stay late, either."

Even as he talked, Leila stood and shrugged off the cardigan she wore to keep warm in the chilly air-conditioned office. The cotton knit fell weightlessly to her chair. Underneath, she wore a sleeveless mini-dress.

Was it her imagination or had his eyes faithfully followed her every gesture?

She grabbed her purse. "I don't have kids." *And I'm not Monica.*

"Then let's go."

From the reception desk, Emilia waived them off with a wry little smile. And while they waited for the elevator, Leila explained that no one had told her she'd have a chance to visit properties or do anything other than answer the phone and manage his calendar. She was grateful for the chance to get out on the field, so to speak.

"It helps if you know what I'm working on," he said. "I make most of my decisions on site."

The elevator opened. Nick pressed G for garage.

"Don't worry. I'm very flexible." The doors slammed shut. Nick studied her with those keenly perceptive eyes but said nothing. She felt the need to clarify. "Meaning I can work long hours."

"Sure."

They rode in silence. A FedEx deliveryman joined them on the ninth floor and got off on the sixth. When they were alone again, Nick said, "Leila is an uncommon name."

"It means 'born at night.'"

"Were you?"

She nodded. "Midnight."

"The bewitching hour."

She smiled. "Clever."

"Amis is French, right?"

She nodded. "You know that because you're from Canada."

"And you're from Florida's west coast."

"How do you know?"

"Your résumé says you went to school in Naples."

"You've read my résumé?"

"Jo-Ann gave it to me."

There wasn't much to her résumé. She was embarrassed by how thin it was: high school and some college. She'd earned her real estate license a year ago, but her only sales experience was in entry-level retail. Leila gripped the handle of her purse to keep from fidgeting nervously. This had to be the longest elevator ride in history.

When they reached the garage, she followed him to his reserved spot. He drove a black Mercedes coupe. She sank into the leather seat and admired the chrome accents of the dashboard. It was all the things her modest Mazda roadster aspired to be but fell short of. She watched as he pressed the ignition button and put the car in reverse.

"This car makes me—"

He stomped on the breaks. "Makes you what?"

Leila grappled for the right word. "Happy. It makes me happy."

"Is that it?"

Was her seat on fire? "What else is there?"

He lifted his foot off the pedal. "Leila, are you into cars?"

God, she loved the way he said her name.

"Sort of. Sure."

"I'm into women who are into cars," he said with a wink. "But don't tell anyone."

The listing was a one-story, mid-century home in Miami Beach's exclusive Bayshore neighborhood. The original layout had been tweaked to appeal to modern tastes. The renovated kitchen opened to an all-purpose living, dining and TV room. All closets and bathrooms had been updated. The showstopper was the yard that backed onto Collins Canal and the dock that could accommodate a decent-size yacht and flatter the ego of any budding millionaire.

While the photographer snapped pictures for the agency's website, Leila tried to imagine the daily routines of the family who'd once lived in the vacated rooms. On a sunny day, they'd probably have breakfast outdoors. Did they throw birthday parties by the pool or spend holiday weekends boating?

"What do you think?" Nick asked.

"I think it's a lovely home."

"Would you like to live here?".

They were in the master bedroom. Leila opened the plantation shutters to admire the water views. "I could get used to this. But how much would it set me back?"

"Four million."

Her heart stopped. "Are you kidding?"

"Why does that surprise you?"

Well, when she thought of *millions*, she thought of *mansions*. This lovely family home was by no stretch a mansion. "You know this same house in any other neighborhood wouldn't cost that much."

"That doesn't change anything." He leaned against the low cherrywood dresser. Every room had a furniture-showroom vibe. "Leila, I need you to believe in the sale."

She laughed. "You've got me confused with a magical fairy."

He grew quiet, a shadow passing over his face.

"It's a joke," she said, worried she'd gone too far.

"I don't think I've heard you laugh before. You're so serious all the time."

"Because I'm trying to impress you, Nick!"

Saying his name had leveled the playing field somehow. They'd swapped the rigid employee-boss dynamic for something looser, less defined. Something trickier. And Nick hadn't missed it. His face lit up with satisfaction.

"Could you stop trying so hard?" he asked.

He hadn't been exactly easy to read or to warm up to. They'd barely exchanged a dozen words since she'd taken the job. Every morning she dressed like an Office Assistant doll, worried she didn't measure up to the ghost of Monica.

"Maybe if I knew what you expected from me…"

"Here's the thing," he said. "I could run my business under a bridge. I don't need an assistant, not really. But I'd like to have someone on my side. Can you be that someone?"

"Good luck getting cell phone reception under a bridge."

He gave her a wry smile. "That's more like it."

The photographer tapped on the open door. "Hey, Nick, I think I'm done."

He left to review the man's work.

Leila leaned against the wall, caught in exquisite turmoil.

She could be that someone.

On the drive back to the office, Nick said he hadn't eaten all day. "There's a place on Washington I like. Would you mind hanging out with me?"

"I don't mind."

This was the perfect opportunity for them to talk. She reached for her phone, sending a quick text to cancel her happy hour plans. She was supposed to meet a guy, a medical resident at Jackson Memorial, whom, after a few chaste dates, she'd started referring to as Dr. No. He was nice enough, but maybe that was the problem.

"If you have plans, I can take you back to the office," he said. "You're off the clock."

"I don't have plans," she replied. "Not anymore, anyway."

"Are you—?"

"Yes, I'm sure. I'd rather have dinner with you."

That sounded more personal than she'd intended.

"I'd rather have dinner with you, too."

He said nothing else until they arrived at the restaurant. The hostess greeted Nick by name and showed him to a table on the terrace. He ordered the house burger and a beer. She ordered tuna sliders and a glass of Pinot. They shared an order of parmesan fries and he told her his plans for the Bayshore property.

"The listing goes live tomorrow. I want to hold the broker's open on Thursday night. That house was built for parties. I want a bar by the pool, a DJ, everything."

"I should take notes." Leila reached for her phone, swiped past a text from Dr. No and opened the notepad app. She typed "Thursday, bar by pool, DJ, catering."

"Do you have a caterer in mind?"

"We've used this place before with decent results."

She lowered her hearty slider to her plate and offered some advice. "When I'm trying to look good at a party, the last thing I want is heavy food. Why not *taquitos* and margaritas?"

"I bet you don't have to *try* to look good, Leila."

She took it as a compliment and thanked him.

"How old are you?"

"Old enough to do this job."

He'd caught her off guard and the lame one-liner was all she could come up with. She had a complicated relationship with her age. According to the scoreboard in her mind, she was trailing the home team by a lot. She'd gone from pageant girl to shop girl and now to office temp all in the time that her high school friends had earned advanced degrees and jump-started bona fide careers.

"But are you old enough to drink?" he asked, pointing to her half-empty glass of wine.

"Very funny. I'm twenty-three, soon to be twenty-four." She paused. "Does it matter how old I am?"

"I'm just trying to get to know you."

"Sorry. I'm a little jumpy."

"Don't apologize," he said. "I'm thirty, and I like the tacos idea."

"*Taquitos*." She typed the word into her phone.

"Are you seeing anyone?"

Leila went still and laid down her phone. "That's kind of personal."

"Extremely personal," he said. "Someone should've warned you about me. I'm about to hijack your whole life."

She folded her arms across her chest. "Someone did."

He wiped his mouth with a black cloth napkin. "You can tell me to go to hell at any time."

"You're harmless," she said, even though his eyes said otherwise. "And, yes, I'm dating someone. Sort of."

He didn't ask for specifics, leaving her disappointed. Instead he asked, "Will he mind if you have to work late?"

"I don't know. I don't usually ask a boyfriend before making career moves."

"So, he's a boyfriend."

"I only meant—"

He reminded her that she was under no obligation to

apologize or to explain. She could tell him to go to hell. That option was still open.

"We've got some time," he said, again consulting his watch. "Is there anything you want to ask me?"

She reached for a fry and the opportunity to ask the one question burning inside her. "Whatever happened to Monica?"

He threw his head back and laughed. "How long have you been wondering about that?"

"Since day one."

Nick took a sip of beer. His long fingers had a firm grasp of the frosty glass. "She got into it with Jo-Ann and things went south from there. She should've let me handle it, but Monica won't back down from anything. We were together three years."

Together three years…an odd way to describe a working relationship.

"I doubt we'll be together that long," she said.

"Planning to ditch me?"

"What I really want is to learn the business."

"So this is a short-term thing?"

Leila worked to keep her voice steady. "Does that bother you?"

"I'm fine with it." He leaned closer. "I know you have retail experience. Anything else?"

"No." She'd worked at designer boutiques, selling sunglasses, scarves and handbags.

"Selling is selling," he said. "But what drew you to real estate?"

"My aunt sold her home last spring. Her agent was my age. When I found out what she made in commission… I figure if I can sell pricey handbags, I can definitely sell condos."

"Overpriced handbags."

Leila's hand instinctively went to her overpriced handbag hanging from the arm of her chair. The iconic logo was stamped into the buttery-soft leather. "That's a matter of opinion."

"That's a matter of fact."

"Says the man with a very expensive watch."

He flashed an easy smile. "The watch is an investment."

"Please!"

"We're getting off topic."

"If I can learn the ropes while studying for the exam, that would give me an advantage. The agency has a great reputation."

She'd done her research. Kane & Madison, headquartered in New York City with branches in Miami and Los Angeles, racked up impressive yearly sales. She didn't expect to stay on with the agency. All the associates were seasoned business professionals. But wouldn't it be awesome to someday be the single woman associate who could give the boys a run for their money?

"We've got the best inventory," he said. "And I'll teach you everything I know. How's that?"

That was actually pretty damn nice. "I appreciate it. Really."

He waived down the waiter and handed over a card. "To be clear, you're using me as a stepping stone."

She could kick herself. Why hadn't she kept her big mouth shut? "Is that okay?"

"If you're going to use me, go ahead and use me," he said. "Don't worry about how I feel about it."

Within the span of a meal, he'd shown her that she was way too earnest. Apologizing, explaining, stumbling over her words. She was nowhere as sharp as she believed herself to be.

"You must think I'm really green."

"That's not what I'm thinking."

The bill arrived. He signed it and left a heap of cash as a tip.

"I'm going to be the best assistant you've ever had."

"I don't know," he said. "The bar is really high."

"Don't underestimate me."

"I promise I won't."

Their waiter cleared the table of crumbs but, as far as she was concerned, they were alone in the restaurant.

He asked if there was anything else she wanted to know. Leila would have liked to ask if he was seeing anyone, but came up against the blunt edge of a double standard. He could push the boundaries all he liked, but she'd be dumb to try. She played it safe and asked what had drawn him to real estate.

He took a minute before answering, tapping the table with the credit card held loosely between his thumb and forefinger. "I started out in finance, as an analyst. Made good money. But routine kills."

"You're restless," she said almost without knowing it.

He looked up, surprised. "You're right."

Yes! She clenched her fists under the table, thrilled she'd scored at his game.

Chapter 4

Nick listened as Leila enthusiastically gave him an update on the broker's open house. She'd used a contact list prepared by Monica to call the top local brokers. No invitations were extended; she offered to add them to a restricted guest list.

"It's the fastest way to create a buzz," she said. "Getting on a list—any list—drives people crazy."

They were in his office with coffee. The night before, they'd agreed to daily meetings, if only for a few minutes. Nick was happy for an excuse to sit with her.

"I like the way you think," he said.

"We have fifty confirmed guests."

"That's enough. No one shows up alone, and then it's a big mess."

"I'm going to order the food."

"Get in touch with Sofia Silva for the bar. She sets it up, picks the wine, the whole thing."

Leila jotted down some notes. Then she asked, "Who pays for all this?"

"The agency. Didn't Jo-Ann tell you about our expense account?"

"No. See why these daily meetings are important? There's so much I need to know."

Nick thumbed through his wallet and handed her a corporate credit card. "I'm glad this is productive, but I could talk to you all day."

She looked up from her lists and notes and smiled. He wondered if the feeling was mutual. But there was no time to dig deeper. He had a busy couple of days ahead.

He arrived to the open house with Sofia, the event planner. A little red roadster was parked out front and he hoped it was Leila's. He was impatient to see her again and barely took the time to inspect the house, as he should. It was Sofia who noticed the candles floating on the pool's surface. She asked whose idea it was. He wasn't sure, but it had Leila's delicate fingers all over it.

"You're here."

Leila walked up from behind him. He glanced over his shoulder and caught a glimpse of her in a red dress.

It was going to be a long night.

"Did you do that?" he asked, pointing through the French doors to the pool in full view.

"The candles? Do you mind? When the sun goes down it'll look really nice."

"I don't mind. It's genius."

"I agree. It'll look gorgeous," Sofia said.

Nick had forgotten Sofia. He introduced her to Leila. After she left to help the bartender set up, Nick turned to Leila and said, "I'm starting to think you believe in this sale."

"You made a believer out of me."

They stepped outside and wandered past the pool, toward the seawall.

"I want the focus to be on the canal," Nick said. "I want everyone fantasizing about the boat they can't afford sitting on that dock."

"What's the point in getting the brokers all liquored up?" Leila asked. "I don't get it."

"It's an excuse for a party," Nick said. "Plus, you've got to cozy up to the brokers. They defend the goal."

"So, they eat, drink, look around...and then what?"

"Then they get to work calling their clients." He pulled her aside. "Here are the rules. These are not friends. If they can screw us over, they will. I want you to be your lovely self, show them around, but don't hover. Let them roam free and discover the property on their own terms.

Answer questions honestly, but don't over share. If they push back, direct them to me. They'll try to tear the place down to weaken our hand, but don't let them. We're offering a top-shelf item here, and I'm determined to make this seller some money."

"How did you get this listing, anyway?" she asked. "Did the owner go through the agency?"

"It rarely works that way," Nick said. "I know the owner. He's moving back to DC. The Miami experiment is over."

They stood facing the water. Across the canal, a row of houses rivaled each other in grandeur and stature, each with gigantic boats tethered to their docks. The setting sun splashed everything tangerine.

"Hey," Nick said, "is the Miata out front yours?"

"Yup. That's my ride," she said proudly.

"I had one like it back in the day," he said. "Mine was black."

"Of course."

"How many miles?"

"Around 85K."

"Ah," he said. "You're loyal."

"Are you?" she asked.

There was a glint of mischief in her eyes. He wanted to know that side of her.

"Not really. I kept mine two years. It was my first. Bought it cash."

"I won mine."

"Won it?" he asked. "How? Like in a raffle?"

The more he got to know her, the more interesting she became.

"No, not a raffle," she said.

"A game show? Were you on a game show, Leila?"

"No. I wasn't on a game show."

"Was it a talk show? They give away cars, right?"

She raised her hands and confessed. "I won it in a pageant."

Nick saw her with fresh eyes. Her demeanor, walk, even her smile, all of it very practiced and sure. "Yes. I see it."

Her face crumpled.

"It's a compliment," he assured her.

His phone rang. Before taking the call, he said, "We'll talk later. Put a pin in 'pageant,' because that's where we'll start."

Leila watched Nick walk away, laughing with the caller. What did he see? she wondered. Was she running around town with an invisible tiara on her head? The thought caused her unbearable embarrassment. Tonight, of all nights, she wanted to impress him.

She'd come early to prepare for the party. They'd opted not to hire a DJ but to show off the outdoor sound system, so she hooked an mp3 player up to the stereo. While the caterer set up the food, she had slipped into the guest bathroom, changed out of her jeans and flats, and come out in a ruby-red Diane von Furstenberg wrap dress and heels.

When he'd glanced over his shoulder and caught her staring, a symphony of emotions erupted inside of her. His eyes were as clear as morning, without even a cloud of suspicion or surprise. When he called her simple idea genius, she'd been transported with joy.

Leila didn't have much time to dwell on her feelings because very soon, the guests arrived, seemingly all at once. At first she kept to the margins, too intimidated to speak to anyone. But when approached, she was prepared.

"List price?"

"Four million."

"Is that firm?"

"Very much. We believe it's priced to sell."

"How many bedrooms?"

"Three bedrooms, including a master suite, and three fully renovated bathrooms."

"Square footage?"

"Roughly twenty-eight hundred."

"I need an exact number."

"Two thousand, eight hundred and seventy-three."

"There's no garage. Am I right?"

"There's a carport."

"A four-million-dollar house with a carport? Where does the Bentley go?"

"In the carport. The yacht goes on the dock. Have you seen the boat lift? State-of-the-art."

"Is the seller willing to make any concessions?"

"You'll have to ask Nick."

The last couple of questions were from an agent named Marisol Sanchez. Earlier, Nick had introduced her as an old friend. Marisol stood as tall as Leila and wore cigarette pants and high-heeled pumps to better show off her long legs. Leila wanted to know his definition of the word "friend."

"But he'll likely say no concessions are necessary," Leila added. She couldn't help herself.

"My client will be the judge of that," Marisol said.

The other agents were equally annoying. Leila was shocked by the behavior of these so-called professionals. They trampled the grass, stomped on the newly polished floors and slammed the kitchen cabinet doors. They pointed to hairline cracks in the ceiling and quizzed Leila on the local zoning laws, as if the *only* reason their clients would not put in an offer was because they'd likely want to convert the porch into a Florida room.

The most appalling behavior was from one of the agency's own, Tony Manning. He showed up late.

After chatting with Nick for a while, he came looking

for her. "Nick says you're responsible for this impressive turnout."

Leila took a look around. The party was in full swing. Now that business was out of the way, everyone appeared more relaxed, drinking and munching on *taquitos*. Her job was done.

"How would you like to take on my next open house?" he asked.

"Sorry. Nick keeps me busy."

"I'm sure he does," Tony said wryly. "That might not always be the case, though."

"What do you mean?"

"Just want you to know you can always switch camps."

"Nick's been very nice to me. I wouldn't think of switching."

"I've known that guy a long time. He's a lot of things, but *nice* isn't one of them."

Leila looked him in the eye. "Tonight's signature drink is a classic margarita. Would you like to try it?"

"I can find my way to the bar," Tony said with a snicker. "I always do."

Nick called out to her from the house. "Leila! I need you."

Tony let out a playful whistle. "You heard the man. He needs you."

Leila's gaze swept from Tony to Nick. She was the rope, stretched taut, in their tug-of-war. When she was close enough to see the scowl on Nick's face, she very nearly laughed.

"You needed to see me?"

"That's a careful edit. I said I needed you, period."

"Well, here I am."

"Marisol says you're tough," he said. "I'm impressed. You might be a natural."

His approval raised her two feet above ground. "I think the open house is a success."

"Success is a confirmed offer, but this is a very good start."

The music stopped, Sean Paul's raspy voice cut off mid-chorus, leaving the party din bare like teeth.

"I think the mp3 player died," Leila said. "I'll go check."

"One more thing," he said forcefully. "Be careful around Tony."

She should have known he wouldn't tap-dance around the issue. But she was familiar with guys like Tony and wasn't concerned.

"I can take care of myself, Nick."

"I can take care of you better."

"How is this a competition?"

"Don't you know me?"

"I'm not sure." Who was he? The shark that Jo-Ann and Tony described, or the nice guy who bought her coffee, offered to mentor her and complimented her achievements?

Marisol joined them. "What's going on here?" she asked nastily. "I thought Monica was your one true love."

Nick turned to her. "Monica's gone. Now Leila's the light of my life and if she says we're not willing to make any concessions, it's because we're not."

While a cleaning crew returned the house to its former pristine condition, she and Nick sat at the breakfast bar with a platter of leftover appetizers and three open bottles of wine.

"What if Marisol's buyer doesn't come through?" Leila asked.

Nick filled their glasses. "I already have an offer."

Even before the open house had started, an offer had come through by phone: the call that had saved her from having to regale him with tales of her pageant days. A woman who'd grown up in the house was hoping to raise her kids in it.

"That's so sweet. I'm rooting for her."

"You're rooting for me, remember?" Nick said. "It's a low offer."

"How low?"

"Three point five."

That sounded like a lot of money to Leila.

"This brings us back to our talk. Keyword: pageant."

Up until then, she'd been feeling fine, riding high on the success of her first open house, Nick's approval and even Tony's fit of envy. She had no desire to revisit the past, not when the present was so good.

Nick browsed through his phone and pulled up a photo he'd saved. There she was, on stage, in a yellow bikini and perilously high heels, hair curled and sprayed in place, and gold glitter rubbed into her brown skin. Leila blinked at the photo then scooted off the bar stool, taking her wineglass with her.

She heard him scramble to his feet. "Are you okay?"

"I'm bracing myself for the jokes," she said. "Go ahead."

She'd heard it all. It had become a "first date" ritual, of sorts. The guy would say, "Tell me about yourself." She'd say, "I used to compete in pageants." He'd follow with asking, "So, what's your plan to wipe out hunger?" or "How will you bring about world peace?"

"I wasn't going to make a joke," Nick said. "I think you look good."

"That's not why you showed me that picture. To tell me I look good."

"Leila, look at me. I thought we'd laugh."

"Laugh at *me*."

Nick swore quietly under his breath.

She wasn't ashamed of the photo. Similar photos of her

posing and twirling and strutting on stage would live forever on the web. All she wanted was to forget they existed.

She faced him. "I'm not that girl anymore. I need you to know that."

"Was she so bad?"

"She was looking for a shortcut. And I'm here to work."

At seventeen, she'd been certain she'd found a fast track to fame and fortune. While her friends worked on their SATs, she'd worked on her strut. And now she had nothing to show for it except an aging sports car and pictures on the web.

"You sound like me," he said. "About five years ago."

"Oh, really? Are there pictures of you in a yellow bikini out there in cyberspace?"

He didn't laugh at the joke. "There may be pictures of God knows what. I've screwed up. Partied hard. Wasted money. Crashed a car."

"The Miata?"

He nodded. "I turned it around, though. Switched careers. Ditched my friends. Focused on work."

Leila was too overwhelmed to speak. He understood. That was exactly where she was in life. Ditching bad habits and focusing on work.

"Leila, I'm sorry."

Then his phone rang and the mood changed.

Marisol had an offer, all cash, three million six. Nick jolted into action. Pacing the floor, he told Marisol his client was considering a similar offer from a buyer with sentimental attachment to the property. "She grew up in the house and won't tear it down. I'm guessing your guy is a developer, in it for the waterfront."

Fifteen minutes later, Marisol called back with a better offer: three point seven. Nick wasn't moved. After consulting with his client, he countered. "Four million clean." They argued about comparative pricing, price per square footage and the relative value of a canal with bay access. Nick had Marisol on speaker, so Leila could follow the exchange. "This is your bread and butter," he said to her between calls. "Everything hinges on the negotiation."

Then her own phone chimed with a text message from Dr. No asking if she wanted to catch a late movie. The short answer was hell, no.

Can't. Working late.

She couldn't possibly leave now. Watching Nick in his element, moving the ball down the field, trying to score, was incredibly exciting, better than anything on the big screen.

You work longer hours than I do.

How about tomorrow?

I'm on call tomorrow. Saturday?

Saturday works.

No sooner had she put her phone away than Dr. No was forgotten. Nick had her full attention.

After one hour of furious calls to Marisol, the seller and the sentimental buyer, an agreement was reached. Marisol came up to three point nine, which turned out to be a quarter million more than Nick's client had expected to make. Leila saw Nick transformed, the tension of the night leaving his face and an unfamiliar calm rolling in like night fog. He was in ecstasy.

"I'll need proof of funds," he told Marisol.

"You'll get it, asshole," she said dryly.

Nick let out a low laugh. "I love doing business with you."

"Sure. Say goodnight to your new girlfriend."

Leila rolled her eyes. *Girlfriend? Whatever.*

Nick chucked his phone and took a victory lap around the great room, soliciting a standing ovation from an imaginary crowd. Leila obliged him with a slow clap. When they settled down, she said, "Marisol is tough!"

"She works with developers. There's good money in that. I knew she could go higher, but wanted to hold out for her client. I respect it, but I don't have time for those games."

"Will they tear down this house for sure?"

"You said it yourself. This house in any other neighborhood wouldn't be worth as much. That's a problem."

"I feel sorry for the woman who wanted to raise her kids here."

Nick came to stand before her. "Don't go soft on me now."

Leila held his gaze. The world went silent. For a fleeting second, she thought he might kiss her. If he did, heaven help her, she'd kiss back.

"Are we okay?" he asked.

Her throat tightened. "We're more than that."

He caught the double meaning. She wished she'd chosen her words more carefully, but it was the truth.

"I'm not going to pull a stunt like that again. You're the most interesting person I've met in a while. I don't want to make fun. I want to get to know you."

She wanted to get to know him, too. But could she say that? How would that sound?

"I can't lose you to Tony."

He had to be kidding about Tony. Nicolas Adrian wasn't that insecure. But when she replied, her voice was hoarse. "You're not going to lose me to anyone."

Chapter 5

This should count as a first date. They'd hosted a party, and that beat dinner and a movie. They'd had their first fight. Nick hated to see her upset, but with that crucial milestone out of the way, couldn't they move on to make-up sex?

He wanted to, so badly.

They'd moved outside. It was a dull night. Gray clouds walled off the moon. He was stretched out on a lounge chair. She sat at the pool's edge, legs outstretched and crossed at the ankles.

"My aunt pushed me into it," she said in response to a question he'd forgotten asking. "I came home with a flyer one day and she went nuts. She thought I had a chance."

"It might not have paid off—"

"It didn't," she said bitterly. "A lot of time and money wasted only to place as a runner up when it really counts."

"You won a car. Most kids have to slave away at a fast-food restaurant to afford a used clunker."

To hear her tell it, she'd wasted her entire life. And he suspected she was hanging on to her old car out of pride rather than necessity.

"Tell me you won't look up any more photos."

"I'll tell you whatever you want to hear."

She sighed. "I give up."

He tried to reassure her. "I'm a little obsessed with you. What can I say?"

"I'm really not that interesting."

"I disagree."

She sat straight and solemnly confessed. "I put stock in all the wrong things. It's a thing with me."

He liked that she trusted him enough to share her weaknesses. "And I like complicated women. That's my thing."

"Like Marisol?" she asked.

Talk about territorial.

"Not like Marisol. But wasn't it good to go up against her tonight?"

"So good!"

She smiled. A dimple appeared in her left cheek and vanished. He'd never seen it before. The more he studied her, the more secrets there were to discover.

"Do you think your client spent his nights this way?"

"By the pool?"

She nodded. "Talking."

"Not likely," he said. "Did I mention he's a dick?"

"Then why fight so hard for him?"

"That's the business, Leila."

Just when he was sure she'd written him off as a heartless bastard, she surprised him with a question.

"How does it feel to win?"

"You'll tell me someday."

To most people he was the golden boy, born under a lucky star. "Success follows you," an old boss once told him. Only he knew the effort that he put into building his career, and the skill it required to make it seem effortless. Leila had drive. He had no doubt she'd turn her luck around.

"Why are you single, Nick?"

It seemed that all the earlier questions had been leading to this one.

"Because I want to be."

Such was his nature. He was bloodless in negotiations and unsentimental with women, but to his mind, these were positives. He didn't have a ton of emotional baggage to weigh him down. You only had so many years to fully dedicate to work, and he had no intention of wasting them. He'd seen friends, men and women alike, make the mistake of settling down early only to get bogged down with kids and family obligations. But Leila was a mistake he was very willing to make.

"Have you ever had a broken heart?"

There was real hunger and curiosity in her dark eyes.

"When I was a kid I wanted a dog, but my dad is allergic. He got me fish instead."

She looked confused, but played along. "That's not a fair tradeoff. Fish don't fetch or wag their tails when you get home from school."

"Tell that to a marine biologist."

"I see," she said. "So your dad got you fish and what? You met a girl who also had an aquarium?"

"No. My dad got me fish and they died, surprisingly fast, even by fish standards."

"Did you kill them?"

"I have a heart, Leila."

"What does it beat for?"

Oh, babe...

They locked eyes. She turned away.

"Are you seriously telling me that your biggest heartache was having to flush away a few fish?"

"I'm telling you that I learned very early that I was better off alone. I'm not sure I'm the better for it. Do you understand?"

"More than you know."

"Who broke your heart?" he asked.

"Ah!" She gave his question some thought. "My high school boyfriend stood me up for prom, and that was the end of it. I cried for one month straight. Lost ten pounds. Gained back twenty. I was a mess."

"You're so pretty. Who would stand you up?"

"There's always someone prettier."

She was quiet for a while. Then she gracefully rolled onto her bare feet, stepped into her high heels and approached him. Her dress gathered at the waist with a knot. Untie the knot and there you had it.

"I should get going," she said.

"I'll walk you out."

"No, don't."

He questioned her silently. She fell into a pile of excuses. "It's late. You have to lock up. I can see myself out. I'll see you in the morning. Okay?"

It wasn't okay. Was this how they were going to play it? Circling the well, careful not to fall in. He wasn't cut out for the Romeo-Juliet thing. But he had to let her go. It was past midnight and his self-control was down to the barest of wires.

He stood and faced her. "What did I tell you about worrying about my feelings?"

She looked him in the eye. "It's too late for that."

Chapter 6

Every minute they spent together, Leila felt Nick circling around her, very strategically stripping her of her defenses. As of last night, he knew almost all her secrets and yet she still had questions. Where did he live? What did he do when he wasn't working? Was he really single or just sleeping around? And, the next day, at their morning meeting, a new question popped up. What was the true purpose of all those trips to New York?

Greg had stopped by Nick's office. He was the only other African American at the agency. Despite his frat boy ways, Leila liked him.

"Heard you had a great turnout last night," he said. "I got a client who might be interested."

Leila and Nick were on the couch, reviewing his calendar. Nick said, "Leila, please get Greg up to speed."

Greg looked surprised. "So…what's up, Leila?"

"As of nine o'clock this morning, the Bayshore property is in escrow."

Greg whistled. "Good work, man. Congratulations."

Nick threw up his hands with false modesty. "I try."

"And that's why she wants you back."

Leila waited until Greg had left before asking what he'd meant.

"Who knows?" He turned his attention to the computer tablet resting on his lap.

Her chest tightened with anger. He was lying.

"Want to get out of here?" he asked.

"Oh, yes."

That was all it took. He was forgiven.

Nick had a listing appointment with the owner of a condo on Collins Avenue. It wasn't the sort of meeting he'd take his assistant to, but he'd grab any excuse to be alone with Leila. When he stopped in front of the building located directly across the street from the high-end mall where she used to work, she shook her head and murmured, "Of course."

He pulled up to the valet and cut the engine. "What?"

She pointed to the sign. Bal Harbour Shops. The crisp white letters stood out against a black backdrop. "Maybe I should go say hello to my old boss. You never know. If this real estate thing doesn't work out."

"It'll work out," he said. "You're learning from the best."

He got out of the car and went around to open her door. She stepped out and said, "I thought Tony was the best."

He tried to laugh at the joke, but couldn't. "Now you're trying to start something."

Before they went inside, Nick took a look at the building. It was wide and flat and looked like every other building on the street. They rode an elevator that jerked to a stop on the fifth floor.

"Feels old," he said.

"It's not so bad. The elevator in my building doesn't work half the time."

"Not so bad is not enough," he said. "We're here to appraise the apartment but also the building, and so far I'm not sold."

A few feet down the hall, a woman stepped through a door. "Hey. I thought you were lost."

Nick walked over and shook her hand. Turning to Leila, he said, "Carrie Hill, this is my assistant, Leila Amis."

Carrie was short compared to Leila. She wore a T-shirt and stretchy pants. Her feet were bare.

"Come on in."

Nick ushered Leila ahead of him.

With a sweeping gesture of the hand, Carrie offered up the main room for his inspection. The room felt cramped.

Maybe the furniture was too large. Or maybe it had to do with the retro built-in bar that ate up so much space. The adjacent kitchen had obviously had a facelift with new fixtures and door pulls, but, sadly, it looked dated. The predictable apartment layout might have been saved by the views, but the views were not impressive. If the beach was out there, it was obscured by a row of palm trees.

Carrie opened a door off the hallway. "Guest bath. Updated with a new pedestal sink."

"And the bedroom?" Nick asked.

"In a minute," she said. "My boyfriend's getting dressed. Let's check out the balcony."

They all stepped out onto the narrow balcony and, after a few awkward seconds of silence, stepped back inside. Nick's first impression was confirmed. There wasn't much to see beyond the landscaping.

"I'm thinking somewhere in the mid-eight hundreds," Carrie said.

"Too high," Nick said.

"For Bal Harbour? I don't think so."

"We're across the street from a mall. I bet the day after Christmas it's a holy nightmare."

He was also willing to bet that congestion on the main road was the reason Carrie Hill was selling her one-bedroom "beach front" condo.

She wouldn't back down. "Just last month a unit sold for—"

"Top floor. Better views."

"Okay. What's your number?" she asked, frustrated.

"Somewhere in the high six hundreds."

Carrie's boyfriend came out of the bedroom. His eyes narrowed on Leila. "Hey! I know you."

Nick watched Leila freeze under the man's scrutiny.

"You sold me that wallet."

That was enough chitchat. Nick stepped between them, eclipsing the smaller man altogether.

"I don't have a lot of time," he said. "If we don't agree on price, we don't have to go any further."

Carrie Hill shrugged. "Up to you. You're not the first agent I've spoken to, and I've got plenty more on my list."

"If they say you can get anything close to eight hundred, they're lying."

Carrie's off-duty yoga instructor vibe vanished. She was an estate planner by profession, and her pragmatic side was now showing.

"I invested a lot updating this place."

Nick pointed to the bar. "Invest some more and knock that thing out."

She stiffened. "I think we're done."

Nick gestured for Leila to head to the door. "Call me if you change your mind."

Out in the hall, Leila chastised him. "Can you really talk to clients that way?"

Nick pounded the elevator button. "She's not a client yet."

"Nick, you were rude back there."

"Listen, Miss Congeniality—"

"Hey!"

"Sorry. Couldn't resist."

Maybe she was looking at this from the retail angle, where the customer was king. But that wasn't how he ran things.

"If it's not priced right, it won't move," he explained. "I'm not taking a listing to have it sit on the market. It's my name, my reputation."

"But—"

"She asked for my professional opinion and she got it."

"Okay, but—"

"I call the shots, Leila," he said. "I'll deliver if a client gives me something to work with."

"Okay, I get it. You're the shot caller."

"She can call someone else."

But she didn't. They were waiting for the car to be brought around when his phone rang. He showed her the display. Carrie Hill.

"Yeah, she wants me," he teased.

"Everybody wants you," she said.

A current passed between them. How he wished that were true.

Saturday afternoon, Leila lugged four bags of groceries up three flights of stairs to her apartment. The unit she shared with Alicia faced a courtyard with a basketball hoop. The neighborhood boys were engaged in a clumsy game of pickup basketball. Before she'd left for the supermarket, she'd watched them saunter onto the court, boasting of skills they'd yet to demonstrate. They reminded her of herself.

Alicia was curled up on the couch, clutching a box of Kleenex. Her naturally wavy hair was braided in two messy rows that snaked along her hairline.

"I'm ordering pizza and watching those car chase movies. You know the ones," she said, her voice coarse.

"Which one?" Leila asked. There were seven at last count.

"All of them." Alicia raised the remote like a scepter. "Are you in?"

"Sorry. I have a date."

"Why so down? If I had a date I wouldn't be watching every car chase movie ever made."

"How about I make you some soup?" Leila offered.

"From scratch?"

"From a can! Do I look like your mama?"

"No, thanks. I prefer pizza."

Pizza and a movie sounded tempting after the busy week she'd had, but there was no way she could back out of meeting Dr. No. She showered and dressed, putting extra effort into her appearance to make up for her lack of enthusiasm. She came out of her room in a red halter, skinny jeans and high-heeled sandals, just in time to open the door for the pizza delivery guy.

"Why can't your date pick you up like a gentleman?" Alicia asked. Consulting the delivery guy, who was seventeen tops, she added, "Am I right?"

The boy shrugged.

Leila replied, "He's working late. It would take him too long to get here. It's easier this way."

"And you want your car to make a quick getaway," the boy said. "Am *I* right?"

Alicia tipped the kid. "The truth always comes out of the mouth of babes."

Everyone was onto her. She decided to be more positive, and started by ditching the negative nickname Dr. No. His name was Dr. Carl Knowles. The problem was that she felt obliged to date him. If a young handsome doctor asked you out, every grandmother alive would agree that you had to say yes. She'd dated bad boys and cool guys, it was time she dated a smart man.

They met at a pop-up bar put together by a team of local mixologists. The downtown location had been announced on Twitter only the night before. Carl was waiting at the unmarked entrance, freshly shaved and looking handsome in a striped button-down shirt and black jeans. They had no problems finding seats at the ground-floor bar. But then it didn't take long to realize that most of the action, music and mingling was happening on the second-floor loft. Leila, determined to give the good doctor her full attention, didn't mind at all.

At the bartender's recommendation, they ordered tequila and pineapple cocktails and standard bar food, buffalo wings for him and flatbread pizza for her. In the harsh light of naked bulbs, Carl's wide eyes glowed. His tawny-brown skin was smooth and blemish-free. He kept her entertained with gruesome tales of emergency-room trauma, but something in his tone irked her: the suggestion that his work was more important than hers or, frankly, anyone else's. Nick wasn't exactly saving lives, but he worked hard. Leila took a long sip of her cocktail. Why was she even thinking about Nick?

Her phone, face-up on the bar, buzzed angrily. The display read Trouble. There was her answer. She couldn't stop thinking about him because there was no escaping him. He was at the office. He was on the phone. He was in her dreams at night. He'd promised to hijack her whole life, and he'd kept his word.

Leila grabbed the phone and mouthed an apology. "I have to take this."

Carl was gracious. "That's fine."

She turned away from him and answered. "Hello?"

"Look up."

Even as her heart sank, she raised her eyes, scanning the second-floor loft. It took only a few seconds to spot him—one hand holding a phone to his ear, the other buried in the pocket of faded jeans. His handsome face was partially shadowed.

"Don't stare," he said.

She quickly averted her eyes, aware that Carl was watching her, too.

"I'm leaving for New York tomorrow night and won't be back before Wednesday."

"Thanks for letting me know."

"No problem. Enjoy your night."

"You, too."

"Leila?"

"Yes?"

"You're beautiful. He's a lucky guy."

She looked up again and he was gone, swallowed by the crowd.

Carl cleared his throat in an effort to grab her attention. She politely indulged him, packing the phone away, knowing his luck had run out.

That night, as she undressed, Leila turned Nick's words over in her mind. Of all the things he could have said—"You look beautiful. You're beautiful tonight. You look beautiful in red."—he'd said, *You're beautiful.*

Chapter 7

Nick left the bar, climbed into his car and tore out of the parking lot. It wasn't even ten, but he wasn't going to stick around. He was this close to setting the place on fire. Seeing Leila out with that guy was like swallowing hot coal. From his vantage point on the second-floor loft, they'd seemed like the perfect couple. And that, he'd admit it, scared the hell out of him.

From the start, she'd said she was seeing someone, but he'd chosen not to believe her. He'd ignored her furtive texting when she'd thought he wasn't watching. And he was always watching.

The thing was, he hadn't been seeing anyone since the day they'd met. It wasn't something he'd decided on. At first, he'd made excuses. He was busy. Working. He had no time. Really, he had no interest. He'd been living the life of a monk, tending to a Zen garden of emotions. He didn't recognize himself, so careful and cautious. Part of it was he liked what they had going. He liked working with her and didn't want to mess with that. She made his daily routines special and her enthusiasm was contagious. The other part was more personal. His life wasn't structured to take on any long-term relationship. And she was young, fragile and trying to sort herself out. He didn't want to hurt her. He had to be sure.

He drove up US-1, gradually picking up speed as his anger flared. Leila could put on a show of jealousy from time to time, but his possessiveness could crush hers. She had to know how he felt. It was in all the things he didn't do. Like touch her. He'd never touched her, not even casually. His touch would reveal too much. Like he'd memorized the grain of her skin and knew it by heart.

Nick screeched to a stop at a red light. He thought he could take his time with her. It was a nice change of pace, and he was enjoying it. He thought he had time. He didn't.

Chapter 8

Weeks passed and Nick's absences increased in frequency and length. When he was away, work turned dreary. Leila answered calls, updated monthly reports, surfed the web and watched the clock. She turned down offers to go out to lunch and stayed close to the phone, hoping he'd call with a question, a riddle that only she could solve.

One afternoon she killed time browsing the agency's website. The home page featured a Meet Our Team link that led to the pages of the various office branches. Each page listed the associates by alphabetical order. With a few clicks, she found Nick.

A short bio listed his degrees and area of expertise— luxury residential homes and condominiums—and a few words on his personal background.

> Nicolas Adrian, originally from Toronto, now calls Miami home. He comes to us from the New York office where he exceeded all sales goals. When he is not working, he enjoys water sports and outdoor activities.

Leila wondered if driving a sports car counted as an outdoor activity.

There was a gallery page with pictures taken at company events. She searched for Nick, and each time she spotted him, a tall, slim redhead was nearby. They were never touching, exchanging coy glances or cuddling. But wherever Nick was, there she was, too, looking amazing in silk blouses and pencil skirts, fiery hair long and loose on her back.

I thought Monica was your true love.

Leila left her desk and wandered to the water cooler.

She poured herself a paper cone full of tepid water. She hadn't expected Monica to be Jessica Rabbit in office attire. After Nick had mentioned that his former assistant had kids, twin boys, Leila had subconsciously put her in a nonthreatening box. Which was, she now realized, the most naïve thought she'd ever had. Sure, the woman in the pictures appeared to be a good ten years Nick's senior, but that didn't make a difference. She had legs for days.

Leila crushed the paper cone in her hand. *Stop this!* The man was her boss, not her boyfriend. For all she knew, he had a girlfriend in New York. Why else would he take every opportunity to fly there?

That night Nick called. She was running the shower when her phone, which was always at arm's length, rang.

"Do you have a minute?" he asked. "It's about the expense report."

He never said hello and that was starting to annoy her.

"It's late," she said. "Why are you still thinking about work?"

"I'm always thinking about work. What are you up to?"

She wrapped a towel around her naked body. "Shower. TV."

"You're too young to spend your nights that way."

"You're too young to patronize me."

"Where's your boyfriend tonight?"

"I never said he was my boyfriend."

"What is he then?"

If she closed her eyes, she could touch Nick's face. "He's just a friend."

"Does that friendship come with a benefits package?"

"That's none of your business," she said. "Why aren't you out running New York City?"

"There's still time."

"So, about the expense report?"

"The photographer's invoice is on my desk. I forgot to turn it in. Monica used to remind me."

"I'm *not* Monica!" she snapped.

He didn't respond right away. During the stretch of silence that followed her outburst, she was in agony.

"I know that." His voice was low.

"I'm sorry. I don't know why I said that."

"I think I do."

She heard him laugh, a soft, rumbling laugh, and wished a sinkhole would open up and swallow her live. "Go and have fun. I'll turn in the invoice in the morning."

She tossed the phone onto the bath mat, stepped into the shower and stood, unflinching, in the cold stream. *I'm so screwed.*

Wednesday ended without word from Nick, as did Thursday. He finally returned late Friday, when the office was half empty.

She was at her desk, refreshing her makeup for a last-minute date with Carl that she'd scheduled out of desperation, when the elevator doors noisily parted. She heard the now familiar grinding of suitcase wheels on marble and instinctively lowered the lip-gloss wand, her hands unsteady.

His blue eyes flashed with surprise. "Why are you still here?"

"I'm heading out now. Did you come here straight from the airport?"

He was dressed for travel in dark jeans and a soft blue hooded jacket worn over a white T-shirt.

"I couldn't wait to get back."

"Even with everything New York has going on?"

"I prefer Miami."

He was looking at her appraisingly and a knot formed in her belly. The sleeves of her dress were long, but the hemline was quite high.

"Honestly, I was hoping you'd be here. Are you free tonight?"

The knot tightened. "I had plans. Nothing definitive. Why?"

"I'm meeting clients for dinner at The Forge. Want to come?"

She nodded silently because, yes, of course, she wanted it more than anything.

"Good. I'm going to change."

He wheeled his suitcase into his office and she quickly sent a text message to Carl. She wasn't proud of it; canceling a date via text wasn't cool. But if she called him, Nick would overhear her at her worst, lying to a guy who didn't deserve it.

Bad news. I have to work late.

Carl responded within seconds.

Again? It's Friday.

She used a line often tossed about in the office.

Real estate is 24-7.

Just when she was about to propose an alternate night, Nick appeared at the door in a midnight-blue shirt with onyx buttons.

"Need more time?" He casually rolled up his sleeves.

She hid her phone, as if caught texting in class. "Just a second."

He started to walk away then stopped. "Leila?"

"Hmm?"

"Tell him you're not interested."

Stunned, she went quiet for a minute. "How do you know that I'm not?"

"I see the way you look at me."

Nick had returned to his office as if nothing had happened, as if he hadn't just drawn blood.

Leila got up, walked down the hall and locked herself in a bathroom stall. Her breath was trapped in her lungs.

What did she expect? She swam with the shark. She got bit.

Chapter 9

They took his car to the restaurant, driving along Arthur Godfrey Road in stiff silence. *I see the way you look at me.* Now she wished she'd never laid eyes on him. So maybe she'd been foolish enough to toss a longing glance his way, it didn't give him the right to call her out so bluntly, arrogantly. Dinner promised to be painful. She didn't know if she could sit through it. She couldn't even look at him.

But Nick broke through the awkwardness in his characteristic way. After pulling up to The Forge and leaving the car with the valet, he turned to her—all business. He was once again her mentor. "I like to meet with new or prospective clients for dinner to get to know them, get a feel for what they're looking for. Always pick a restaurant you think they'll like. If they drink, keep their glasses full. And let them do the talking. Tonight we're meeting a creative couple, interior designers. They should love this place."

"Who pays for dinner?" she asked.

"You do, love. Always."

She flinched at the endearment. The doorman held open the heavy wood door. Leila grabbed Nick by the sleeve and tugged him to the side.

"Listen. I'm sorry if I led you to think—"

He silenced her with one hard look. "Don't do that."

"You don't get it. I'm dying inside."

In a move she hadn't anticipated, he grabbed her hand, squeezed it. A current of electricity ran up her arm. It occurred to her right then he'd never touched her, not even casually.

"We'll talk after dinner," he said. "Now, let's work."

She could tell that, for him, the matter was resolved. It wasn't. Yes, she'd skirted the edge and gotten dangerously close to tipping over. Even so, she had enough common sense left over to find her way back to safety.

Belgian designers Edouard Bonneville and Christophe Le Grand—Eddy and Chris— were in high spirits when they were escorted to their table, cheeks rosy with a champagne flush.

Nick's restaurant choice was perfect. From the moment they'd stepped through the doors, Leila was enthralled. The pairing of traditional stained-glass windows and whimsical lilac chandeliers blew her away. And she couldn't get over her grand, upholstered wing chair. She felt like she was hosting a tea party in Wonderland. With plates piled with steak, shrimp and the most exotic salads, the three men discussed travel, traffic, nightlife—anything but real estate. They were halfway through Limoncello cheesecake when Eddy brought up the house hunt. Or rather, the hunt for the perfect South Beach—"Sobe"—condo.

"It has to be a showstopper," Eddy said. "How else will our clients know they can trust us?"

Chris wasn't worried about clients. "Easy access to the beach is a must. We want the full Sobe experience."

"We want the full Sobe experience in a condo we can later sell for a profit," Eddy specified.

"I understand," Nick said. "And I know just what you're looking for."

"Eddy and I have been together for seven years," Chris said. "We've lived all over the world, but we're most at home in Miami. It's a crazy city, an infuriating city, but we love it."

Nick said he felt the same way. He explained that as a child of typical Canadian snowbirds, he'd spent many winter breaks in South Florida. "The first time around we spent a couple weeks right here on the beach. My folks hated it. It was pricey, touristy, and they couldn't get away fast enough. After that, they rented trailers in Hollywood. But I moved to South Beach the minute I could."

Chris and Eddy stared at Nick in shock at the mention of trailers. Leila was equally moved but for a different reason. This was the first time he'd spontaneously shared a personal anecdote.

"How long have you two been together?" Eddy asked.

Nick pointed to Leila with his fork loaded with the last bite of cheesecake, and Eddy nodded.

"We're not together." Leila spoke up for the first time that evening. "Tell them, Nick."

"Tell them what?" His eyes challenged her.

Leila felt outnumbered. "That we only *work* together."

"I don't know, Eddy," Chris said. "Sounds complicated."

"Let's check back on these two in a few weeks," Eddy said, "and see if the story changes."

Chris was delighted. "We're designers, but we're also matchmakers. All we need is a reality show."

Nick wrangled the stray horses. "How about we focus on getting you two into a kickass condo in a few weeks?"

The couple was holding hands. Eddy said, "You came highly recommended. We expect magic."

"I'll give you magic," Nick said. "But first let's talk money."

The two "couples" parted ways at the door. Chris and Eddy walked out into the crisp late-October night and Leila was only steps behind them when Nick took hold of her arm and led her to the bar. It was decidedly less crowded now that the happy hour was officially over. He ordered two glasses of champagne. The bartender held up a bottle of Veuve Clicquot and he approved.

Leila slipped onto a bar stool, taking care to avoid a wardrobe malfunction by strategically crossing her legs. Her maneuvering appeared to amuse Nick. He watched her with a smile, the silver shimmer of the domed ceiling reflected in his eyes. All evening, she'd noticed the way women—gorgeous women, rich women—eyed him. Secretly she'd wished they really were together.

"We have to talk," he said matter-of-factly.

No kidding. She took the lead. "We work together. We can't mess that up."

"We won't be working together for long."

That was fair. She'd told him about her plans for the future. The thing was, she liked working with him. This was the first job she'd ever enjoyed and was in no hurry to quit. "We don't know that."

"Yes, we do. I'm moving back to New York to help set up a new sales team."

Leila felt suddenly dizzy. She rested her champagne flute on the bar, afraid that she might drop it.

"Connie Madison is asking me to do it as a personal favor. Her lead associate quit to join the competition."

Connie Madison—as in Kane & Madison Realty. This was the woman who wanted him back.

"It's the offer of a lifetime, Leila. And a chance to rake it in."

"Money," she said flatly.

He nodded.

She turned away. Now something else was clear—all the hints that Tony and Greg had dropped. Everyone had been clued in about this. She stared at Nick, knowing that he'd purposely hid it from her. "You've known this for a while."

"Nothing concrete."

"You lied to me."

"I withheld information, Leila," he said firmly. "Until I was sure."

Leila used her last reserves of courage to offer a smile and encouragement. She couldn't let him see how much it hurt. "Nobody ever complained about having to move to Manhattan for a great job. Congratulations."

"That's true, but the timing is off." He pushed aside his champagne glass and ordered a whiskey straight. "I don't want you to worry. I spoke to Jo-Ann and made sure she'll keep you on. We had it out, but that's okay."

"You told *Jo-Ann* before me?"

Her outburst was ridiculous. Jo-Ann *was* the office manager, after all. But Leila was swimming in deep panic now. In the short time that she'd known him, only three months, really, she'd invested everything in him. She couldn't remember how she'd spent her days before him.

"I called her from the plane. I had to know what to tell you."

"When do you leave?"

"In eight weeks."

He had to be settled and ready to work straight after the new year.

"Why is the timing off? Is there something else at play?"

"You are," he said. "And don't pretend you don't know it."

What did it matter now? What had once seemed vital, crucial, was crushed to nothing. "Forget me. The last thing I want to be is dead weight."

"Dead weight?" Nick laid a hand on her bare knee. "Leila, you're the prize."

She closed her eyes. Everything she felt for him, a fluid mix of admiration and lust, rushed to the forefront. She was certain that everyone, including the bartender, could see her drown.

He leaned closer and spoke into her ear. "Sorry if I'm not playing fair. I don't care if there are rules against this. I want you. I *know* you want me. How long do we have to dance around this?"

Not long. Leila, having made up her mind, finished her champagne and slid off the bar stool. It was time to jump down the rabbit hole.

"Come." She took his hand. "You have me for eight weeks."

Chapter 10

Nick tipped the valet and, hardtop down, tore through the carnival streets of South Beach at night. With Leila beside him, hair flapping in the wind, he doubted any man was happier tonight. He took the causeway toward the Venetian Islands. He lived in a gated community on the waterfront. Rather than waste time driving to the residents' garage, he parked in an open lot. He took Leila by the hand and they raced into the building, feet pounding on the cobblestone walkway.

Nick greeted the security guard in the brightly lit lobby. The elevator was empty. He pressed the button marked seven. She joked, "Lucky seven." He didn't laugh. He backed her into a corner wanting to steal that first kiss. But she pointed to the glass eye of a camera.

"Careful," she said. "We're being watched."

"I don't care." He gripped the hem of her dress, inching it higher. "You didn't wear this dress for me."

"Why does it matter? You get to take it off."

"It matters. Were you going to meet him tonight?"

"Who?"

"Your boyfriend."

"For the hundredth time, he's not my boyfriend. Although, if I had any sense he would be. He's an awesome doctor and a good person. He saves lives."

"Even if he'd saved my life, I'd still want him out of your life."

Leila touched his face and playfully reminded him of the terms of their agreement. "You get eight weeks. After that, it's anybody's game."

"We'll see," he said. "You don't know what you've gotten yourself into."

She looked up at him, brown eyes shining. "I think I do."

Nick ushered her down the hall and into his condo. Once the door was closed behind them, he grabbed hold of her shoulders, swept her hair out of the way and yanked on the pull of her dress zipper. Cold air pouring out the overhead vent caused her exposed back to erupt in bumps. He turned her around to face him, giving her one last chance to back out.

She wrapped her arms around his neck. "Eight weeks, Nick. You're wasting time."

He thought he might crush her with his kiss, but she rose to it again and again. With the first taste of her, he forgot everything that wasn't her. The feel of her in his arms. Her scent. She moaned and the deep soulful sound filled his ears.

Then the security alarm sounded, the most annoying, ear-piercing beeping that made her jump. Nick muttered, "Shit!" He released her to punch a code into a keypad near the door. "You make me forget everything."

"Don't blame me."

His phone rang. While he reassured the security guard that he wasn't a victim of a home invasion, Leila escaped him. She ventured deeper into the apartment, seemingly drawn to the view of the bay, the inky-black water reflecting a rainbow of city lights. Nick ended the call and silenced the ringer. He watched fascinated as she slipped out of her dress. It fell to a ring at her feet and she stepped out of it.

"Turn around."

She did as she was asked. She was more beautiful than he could have ever imagined. That rich brown skin, those breasts beautifully packaged in lace. Those legs.

Then it hit him.

"You wore that for him?"

She opened wide eyes. "That's your reaction?"

"Sorry, but—"

"But what? Were you expecting Fruit of the Loom?"

"It's just—"

"Nick, I worked at a luxury shopping mall for a long time. This is all I own. Get used to it."

"You're telling me you wear lace every day?"

"Except laundry day, of course."

He went to her, tucked a finger under the waistband of her panties. "Be honest. Is this why you can't afford a new car?"

She spoke through clenched teeth. "You're killing the mood with these questions."

"Am I?" He fit his hand between her legs and ran his fingers along the delicate lace, finding it damp. He leaned closer and kissed her neck. "I'm going to be imagining what you've got on under your clothes every day from here on out."

"I hope so."

Nick snapped open her bra and found the pretty lace thing fell away effortlessly. He cupped her breasts and rubbed the pad of his thumbs against the nipples, forcing them awake. But he kept his eyes on her face. Brows drawn, eyes hooded and lips parted. She was so sexy.

"Leila, you're going to make me very happy for eight weeks."

"Nick, your happiness is out of my hands."

He took her delicate hand in his and placed it firmly on his erection. "I disagree. It's very much in your hands."

She squeezed mercilessly. "I think you're overdressed."

Nick took care of that in less than a minute. Then he scooped her up, carried her to the bedroom and tossed her onto the bed. He went to the bathroom for a condom and found her sitting up in bed.

"Tell me there's no one else. I'm the only one."

The seriousness of her tone gave him pause. She'd been so playful a moment earlier.

"What are you worried about?"

"Just answer me."

He swept her hair away from her face. "Leila, there's only you."

She could take that any way she wanted. There was only her. No one mattered. No one else existed.

She rose onto her knees, took the foil packet from his hand and ripped it open with her teeth. He watched her work the latex over him.

For whatever reason, Nick had not imagined what type of lover she might be. For sure, he thought she might be shy. *This* Leila, he wasn't prepared for. It both aroused and challenged him. And he loved nothing more than a challenge.

Nick took her by the waist, swept her off the bed and onto the floor. He climbed on top of her, kissed her and whispered hoarsely, "Wrap those legs around me."

She opened to him and Nick's longing for her receded and came crashing down on him. All those days. Those nights away from her. The torture of having her near, but needing to keep her at arm's length. To be inside her now... To feel her soft and hot around him...

Leila clung to him and pressed her face to his chest. Nick eased her away and pinned her arms over her head.

This was no time to be shy.

"You want me. Here I am."

He started to move. She bit her lip, muffling a cry. He wanted to hear her.

"You've thought about me? Tell me."

"*Yes*," she hissed.

"When? Where?"

"All day. All the time."

He kissed her again. "It's relentless this thing between us."

She moaned and tried in vain to wiggle her arms free.

Frustrated, she tightened around him. Her legs circled his waist and he dove deep inside her.

"I'm your lover, baby. It's you and me and no one else."

Nick released her arms and she flung them around him, gripped him tight, calling out his name while she came.

Leila inspected her body in the bathroom mirror, astonished that it wasn't bruised after the demands of love. Her eyes were rimmed with smeared black liner but otherwise she was intact. She raked her fingers through her tangled hair, rinsed with mouthwash and scrubbed away the makeup with a damp towel. She did all this without actually confronting her reflection, afraid of what she might see. Ever since she'd met Nick, she had the feeling of driving blindfolded. A crash was inevitable. The proof was in the mirror.

In the bedroom, blackout drapes held back the dawn. Nick was seated at the edge of the bed, his head low. His naked body was lean, his legs stretched out before him. He reached blindly for her and, when she was close enough, buried his nose in her naval. She stroked his hair, letting her hands travel along the length of his spine. His fingers found her sleek and ready, but still he stroked her until she let out a low cry. Then he took hold of her hips and guided her on top of him. She gasped, astonished, once again, by how well they fit. His fingers dug into her flesh. He controlled the rhythm. He controlled her.

She was fooling herself. There'd be no getting over Nick. Not in eight weeks. Not ever.

Chapter 11

Nick left her asleep, returning a half hour later with breakfast and coffee. He found her on the balcony in one of his T-shirts and little else. Her back to him, she leaned gracefully over the rail, arching her back to better take in the view of the bay dotted with white sailboats. He tapped on the door; she glanced over her shoulder.

He yanked open the door, walked over and kissed her hungrily. She reciprocated in kind. It was one of the things that had struck him. How generous she was with herself. All night she'd trusted him, had followed his lead without question. And he'd led her down some tortuous paths.

"Why would you leave a stranger alone in your apartment?" she asked. "I went through your medicine cabinet."

"You're not a stranger," he said, setting up the food on the low table. "I know where you work."

She blinked as if she didn't know what to do with the fork and knife he'd handed her. "Did you hear me? I went through your medicine cabinet."

"So what? There's nothing in there...except Advil and condoms."

That made her laugh. "So many condoms! You can't be having that much sex."

"Don't challenge me on that." He stirred his coffee. "What else did you find?"

"Your collection of suits."

"You went through my closet?"

"I was looking for something to wear."

"A warrior needs armor. What else?"

"Your bike and fishing rods. I didn't know you fished."

"Those things are in plain view. You can do better than that."

"I wasn't *snooping*."

He handed her a fresh bagel. "Of course not."

"Okay, well…" she said, going for the bonus round. "You read spy novels. A whole lot of John le Carré."

"It's a good way to kill time on a plane."

"I figured you read *Forbes* or *Fortune*."

"I figured you'd figure that. Anything else?"

She pointed to the pristine stainless-steel barbecue in a remote corner of the balcony. "You don't grill."

"That came with the place." He grinned. "You were a busy, busy girl."

Leila curled up on the daybed they shared. The breeze ruffled her hair and her brown eyes were clear. She was a gorgeous creature.

"All in all, I really like your place."

"Thanks."

"Have you always lived here alone?" she asked innocently, spreading cream cheese on her bagel.

"Always. It's been my own little Bat Cave."

"How will you give it up?"

"You know what they say about rolling stones."

Her face clouded with sadness and it broke his heart.

"You know," she said, "at some point you'll have to take me back to the office so I can pick up my car."

He ran a hand down the length of her leg. "We are nowhere near that point."

"If you're not going to take me back—"

"I'm not."

"Then you're going to have to tell me something about yourself. Something real."

"How do you mean?"

"I don't know anything about you except what's in your bio.

"You looked up my bio?"

"No."

"Leila, you're not as good a liar as you think."

"It's right there on the agency's home page. I didn't *look* it up."

"What do you want to know?"

"Anything!" she cried out, frustrated. "Give me *something*. I don't know. Tell me about your childhood, your parents."

"My folks are academics, a couple of marine biologists," he said. "Which means I grew up eating a lot of mac and cheese. Not one of them could cook worth a damn. Apparently, I was some kind of whiz—"

"A prodigy?"

"I wouldn't go that far. I tested well. Won things."

"Like what?"

"Blue ribbons at science fairs, first place at spelling bees and speed-cubing. I was ace at speed-cubing."

"What the hell is that?"

"It's a competition where the fastest kid to solve the Rubik's Cube wins."

"I could never figure out that stupid cube. How do you even do that?"

"The possibilities are limited," he said. "You work them out and lock them down."

He reached over and brushed a crumb from the corner of her mouth. She surprised him by grabbing his hand and kissing the palm.

"If you're as smart as you say, why aren't you busy building a better mousetrap or something?"

"Wait. Is my mother paying you?"

"Well?"

"My parents spent their lives studying algae. Their research depends on grants. They drive an old truck and live in a shell of a house. Every winter I worry they may freeze to death. If I were interested in algae, I'd have built a lab and made millions off the stuff. We're different people."

"But they're proud of you. They've got to be."

He wasn't certain. "They don't get what I do or why I do it. They're not motivated by money."

"Money's not your only motivation," she said, looking at him over the rim of her coffee cup. Her thick lashes couldn't hide the spark of curiosity in her eyes.

"You've seen my car. You know what I'm about."

"Yes." She leaned in and kissed him. "And I think it's hot."

He welcomed the kiss but he wouldn't be distracted. "Your turn. Go."

She shifted uncomfortably. "Where do I start?"

"With your parents. How did they screw you up?"

"Well, my father is from Haiti, so I grew up eating a lot of rice and beans."

"What do they do? Where are they now?"

"In a better place."

Nick took a moment to absorb her words. "Baby, I'm sorry—"

She waived away his concerns. "It was a long time ago."

Nick reached for her and drew her to him. He wasn't fooled. Feigning detachment from her past was probably the only way she could live with it. "What happened?"

"Two things happened."

He said nothing, waited for more.

"My dad worked construction. He had an accident on site. Some scaffolding fell. A few months later, he died of complications. So my mom and I left Miami to join my aunt in Naples. My aunt had found work in the resorts and my mother thought she could, too. One Saturday morning, for no reason that I can remember, Mom decided to drive down to Miami. They believe she fell asleep at the wheel."

"Were you with her?" He would hate to think she'd lived through that kind of trauma.

"I had a cold, but pretended to be worse off than I was. I stayed behind with my aunt and spent the morning trying on her clothes."

"That's okay," he said. "You were spared."

"It's not okay. Not really."

"Leila…"

"I picked my aunt over my mother."

"That's not what you did. You ducked out of a boring road trip. What kid wouldn't?"

She paused. "When I say my aunt found work at the resorts, I mean she managed the spa. She's my mother's sister and very beautiful. My mom worked housekeeping. She had to push that heavy cart down the hotel halls…" Her voice trailed off. "She wasn't the hotel spa type. I was twelve and I wished she was."

"Leila, you were a kid," he reminded her.

Just then his phone rang, offering them a reprieve. He took the call in the kitchen, pacing the hardwood floor. His eyes never left her. She looked so fragile, curled up in a ball, hugging her knees. He wanted to protect her from her past, her own negative thoughts and the world.

After breakfast, Nick rested his head on her lap with a laptop balanced on his chest. While he scrolled through real-estate listings, searching for options for Chris and Eddy, she raked his hair. All he could think was that she was his for eight sex-filled weeks—minus one day.

He'd limited the search to properties located south of Fifth Street, the most exclusive strip on South Beach. Leila was astonished at the seven-figure prices.

"Are you kidding me?" she cried. "Can they afford that?"

"They'd better be able to."

At dinner, the couple had left the budget open. Clearly, she hadn't understood what that meant.

They studied photos and videos of artfully staged rooms. He pointed out the wealth of amenities: gym rooms, tennis courts, valet services and Olympic-size swimming pools. He picked a thirteen-hundred-square-foot apartment on South Pointe Drive. List price: one million five. "What do you think about this one?"

She looked over the photos. "Kind of plain, but it might work."

"The location is right on the money."

"I guess it's worth a look."

He glanced up at her. "Hunting listings with you is the sexiest thing I've done with a half-naked woman."

She pinched his nose. "You Canadians live sheltered lives."

"Want to go see it?"

"Now?"

"Sure. I'll give the agent a call. She's a friend."

"Oh, I'm sure she's a friend," she said harshly. "I can't go. I need a change of clothes."

"There's a shop down the road."

"I'm particular about clothes," she said. "I don't want to spend money on an outfit I'll never wear again."

"It's on me."

"You're not buying me clothes. This is not a scene from *Pretty Woman*. Just take me to my car."

Nick pressed for what he wanted. "I'll take you to your car, follow you to your place and wait for you to change."

"How about you give me a couple of hours and I'll meet you wherever you want."

"I'll give you three hours, but we'll meet right here. Pack a bag. Take everything you need. You're spending the weekend with me."

Chapter 12

The listing agent had agreed to meet them at four in the afternoon. Leila recognized her from the open house. Her name was Raquel Garcia, a brunette with an injection-filled pout. She was happy to see Nick—and only Nick.

"Nice of you to tag along, Leila."

Before last night, Leila would have ignored her. But Nick was hers now—hers. This endless parade of snarky women grated on her nerves. She was about to say something equally caustic when Nick stepped in.

"A simple hello would've worked."

Raquel put on a show of indignation. "I didn't mean anything by it."

"Sure you did. I'd be disappointed if you didn't."

Raquel huffed. "Let's just do this."

The building's lobby was all polished stone and glass. A wall fountain made soothing sounds. They rode up to the fifteenth floor and followed Raquel down a hallway that doubled as a gallery space for modern sculpture.

The condo unit itself was no bigger than the apartment Leila shared with Alicia. Unlike her apartment, the unit had a modern feel. The floor was a honey-toned bamboo. Raquel pointed out that the wall between the guest bedroom and living room had been replaced with glass panels for "flexibility." Also missing was the upper kitchen cabinets, which made the space seem larger than it was but arguably less functional. The master bedroom was nothing special, but the en suite bath and walk-in closets had all the bells and whistles anyone could hope for.

After the tour, Raquel waited in the living room while Leila and Nick stepped out onto the balcony to talk. They leaned on the iron balustrade. The view of the beach would satisfy both Chris and Eddy.

"Do me a favor," Nick said. "Raquel is watching. Pretend you hate it."

"I don't have to pretend," Leila said. "It has no character. Your place is much better than this."

"Well, thank you, babe."

"How is it worth a million and a half?"

Nick turned to the view and pointed to Government Cut in the distance.

"The view alone can't be worth that much. I thought after the market crashed—"

"You thought prices might be fair?"

"Not fair, but reasonable. Accessible."

Again he pointed to Government Cut.

"Yes, I know! I get it!" she cried. "We're South of Fifth."

"Bottle that outrage for when we tour McMansions out in Homestead."

"Like you'd ever be caught dead in Homestead. Chris and Eddy deserve more for their money. You should keep looking."

"*We* should keep looking. You're in this now." He hooked a finger through the belt loop of her jeans and reeled her in. "The hunt continues."

She nudged him. "You said your parents aren't motivated by money. Neither are you."

"You keep trying to redeem me," he said. "Nothing wrong with money, Leila. It's the currency of power."

"I read that quote on the internet somewhere."

"Okay, smarty, what's my motivation?"

"The deal," she said. "You like lining up the pins and knocking them down. That's what excites you."

Nick tilted his head. "Want to talk about something that really excites me?"

"No," she said firmly. "Raquel is watching, remember? Everybody already thinks we're sleeping together."

"Good thing we are," Nick said. "Don't want to mislead anyone."

"Okay," she said, "then why not start with me? I think you've slept with everyone you've ever worked with. Am I wrong?"

"Excluding Greg and Tony, you mean."

"I'm serious."

"So am I."

"Did you sleep with Raquel?"

"Not if memory serves."

"You don't remember?"

"We might've fooled around in the back seat of her Escalade."

The scene flashed before her eyes: Nick and Raquel intertwined, her skirt hiked up to her waist.

"It was just for fun," he said.

As if that made it any better.

"Have you had any serious girlfriends?"

"Depends on what you mean by 'serious' and 'girlfriend.'"

"You're not a relationship person."

"Who is, Leila?"

"Lots of people. Most people."

Nick waved her words away. "Most people make choices when the time is right. To be honest, I'm focused on my career."

Eight weeks, she reminded herself. Maybe the universe had set it up this way to protect her from certain heartbreak.

"What about you?" he asked. "Is there some great love in your past? I don't mean your prom date."

Leila opened her mouth to respond but found she couldn't remember the name of the guy in college she'd been so infatuated with.

Then, likely tired of being ignored, Raquel joined them

on the balcony. "If this doesn't do it for you, I have something else in the building. It's not on the market yet, but the owners are home and willing to let us in."

The unlisted condo was a corner unit on the thirtieth floor. The owners, a married couple in their eighties, explained that it broke their hearts to leave the home they'd purchased for their retirement but they had no choice. Leila understood all too well, having had to walk her aunt Camille through a similar process.

The couple waited in the hall while Raquel showed Nick and Leila around. The interior was a chaotic mess of faux stone finishes, smoky mirrors and heavy drapes. The kitchen was of another era and would have to be gutted. The master bathroom with its bidet, walk-in tub and grab bars was not suited for a young, hip couple. But Leila had a feeling they'd hit gold. Nearly every room, including the dated bathroom, offered water views. And the fact that the space hadn't been updated meant that Chris and Eddy, talented designers, could go wild.

"What do you think?" Raquel asked.

"It's not exactly turnkey," Nick said.

Raquel bristled. "I know. We're discussing staging options."

"Save your money. Staging isn't going to save this."

"It's an amazing space and you know it."

"Let's talk price."

"Two point two."

Nick winced. "Ouch!"

"What's the problem? You can see Fisher Island from the freaking john."

"This place has to be gutted, down to the studs."

"In the right hands, it'll be a showstopper. We know it, and we're not going to give it away."

Nick turned to Leila. "What do you think?"

Leila measured her words. "It has potential, but will Eddy see it? I'm not sure."

"Don't you dare tag-team me," Raquel said. "I know what you're up to."

Nick laughed. "Raquel, you used to love dealing with me. Where did we go wrong?"

Raquel was stone-faced. "Clearly, you love *dealing* with someone else now."

And Leila loved *dealing* with Nick, as much as she loved the time they carved out to be alone together. If they weren't making love, somewhere, anywhere they could manage, and not be caught, they were talking about work. They searched listings, attended open houses, analyzed comparative pricing and discussed market trends.

When Chris and Eddy put an offer on the condo with views from the freaking john, they celebrated like some couples might celebrate a milestone anniversary. Nick took her to dinner. They dined on candy-shaped ravioli and never once checked over their shoulder to see who might also be in the cozy Italian restaurant.

Even with his transfer imminent, Nick went on previewing properties, booking appointments and courting clients. The man never stopped working. His drive made him all the more alluring. Leila couldn't keep her eyes off him.

The tight confines of the office made matters worse. Keeping up appearances was a struggle, which shouldn't have been the case, considering she was trained in the art of masking inner turmoil with bright eyes and a broad smile. But Nick robbed her of her tools and tricks. She was giddy around him, light-headed. She laughed too loudly and looked a little too content at work. She worried she wasn't fooling anyone and that Nick wasn't even trying.

She scolded him one afternoon when he followed her

into the office supply room. "We're supposed to be on the low. Do you know what that means?"

"I'm familiar with the concept."

"You can't follow me around like this."

He locked the door. "I can't help myself."

"You're going to get us in trouble."

He had her trapped against the shelf stacked with ink cartridges and sticky pads. "Kiss me and I'll leave."

"I can't. You'll have red lipstick all over your face."

"You leave me no choice."

She was wearing her pleated skirt, the one she'd worn on her first day. He'd said it drove him crazy. The flared hem allowed easy access. He bent before her, the soft fabric draped over his shoulders. She bit down on a sticky pad to keep from crying. There was no fighting it. She just couldn't help herself.

Chapter 13

One Friday in mid November, Nick called her at the office, claiming to have back-to-back listing appointments. He'd be out all day. Holding the phone to her ear, she checked his calendar. It was blank. He suggested dinner, but couldn't fully commit. He'd call her back around five to confirm. "Maybe we could meet somewhere at seven."

Leila, feeling slighted, rejected the invitation outright. "I think I'll stay in tonight."

He did not press her. "Let me know if you change your mind."

She replaced the receiver and took a sip of water to settle her stomach. Relationships were roller coaster rides, the highs giving way to sudden drops. She'd expected as much. But on her birthday?

No, she hadn't made the grand birthday announcement. She had planned to whisper it in his ear in bed right before requesting the gift of multiple orgasms. Now that plan was shot. More importantly, though, when had they taken this turn? Usually she could see the signs: one-sided conversations, missed calls, text messages gone unanswered. Just last night he'd covered her naked body with hot kisses, as if branding it as his own. Tonight, he couldn't squeeze her in for dinner.

Leila was having a lonely lunch at her desk when Jo-Ann stopped by to give her the afternoon off. "Nick's gone," she said. "It's Friday. Go have fun."

Leila tried thanking Jo-Ann, but she waved it off. "Don't thank me."

During the slow elevator ride to the garage, she considered Jo-Ann's choice of words. *Nick's gone.* Not "gone for the day." Just gone. They were probably already interviewing candidates to fill his position. Everyone was getting ready for life after Nick—everyone except her. She was running full-speed toward the cliff.

Go have fun. It was Friday in a city that lived for the weekend, and she was drawing a blank. Leila couldn't recall the things she'd liked to do before Nick, or even the phone numbers of friends she used to hang out with. There was always the sales team at the boutique. She hadn't heard from them in a while. Maybe she'd stop by for a visit, treat herself to a decent lunch and spend the afternoon window-shopping. Or actual shopping. It was her birthday, after all.

Leila absently got off the elevator on the wrong floor and had to take the stairs to get to her car. When she spotted the Miata, the first thing she noticed was a large red envelope tucked under the windshield wiper. It contained a first-class ticket to New York City and a brief note reading, "Meet me at LGA, Centurion Lounge, 7:00 p.m." There were additional instructions for her to check the trunk of the car.

She popped open the trunk and discovered an oversize Neiman Marcus box wrapped with a red bow. She tore into it like Christmas, finding a structured black wool coat, a pair of leather gloves and a white cashmere scarf as soft as a cloud. Leila buried her nose in it. More than the thrill of the surprise, she was overwhelmed with relief. Nick wasn't gone. He was right here.

"I'm glad you changed your mind."

The hostess had pointed him out, seated by the windows overlooking the runway where a silver Boeing stood out against a soft lavender sky. *Magnificent.* And she wasn't thinking about the plane.

He rose to greet her, smiling, proud of the coup he'd so seamlessly carried out.

"Happy birthday, love."

After a kiss she asked, "How did you know?"

"Oh, come on."

"What if I hadn't shown up?"

"I'd have someone find you and drag you here."

"How did you get Jo-Ann to—?"

He kissed her again, harder. "Forget Jo-Ann. Forget everything. Can you do that for me?"

"I can try."

He wasn't convinced. "You need a drink."

The menu listed fruity cocktails with Miami-inspired names. "We're heading to Manhattan," Nick told the waitress, rejecting her recommendations—the Five Island Flamingo and the Collins Avenue Collins.

"Off menu, we offer the Astoria Bianco, a classic New York martini with a twist."

"Sounds good," Leila said.

"We'll have two."

While they waited for their cocktails, Nick asked her when she'd last visited New York.

"Five years ago. I was a model at a hair convention in New Jersey."

He massaged his temples, seeking to relieve the pain her words had inflicted. "Stop talking."

"You asked!" she cried. "After the gig, a few girls and I rode the subway into the city. We spent the day shopping."

"What the hell is a hair convention?"

"It's an extravaganza showcasing all the latest styles and trends."

The waitress returned with two martini glasses garnished with orange peels.

Nick proposed a toast. "To New York…done right!"

Leila raised her glass. "To New York!"

The chilled liquid went down smoothly, washing away the day's emotions.

"Name one thing you'd like to do," Nick said.

"I'd love, love, *love* to stroll Fifth Avenue. Tiffany. Berg-dorf. Saks."

"What else?"

"Nick, you've been generous enough. I'm fine spending the day at Central Park."

"Don't do that." He rested his glass on the round table between them and took her hand in his. "Let me spoil you rotten."

"This trip is too much already. Normally, I would—"

"I don't care what you'd normally do," he said. "You're with me. And we're past all that."

That much was true. So when she woke up the next morning in a smart hotel suite overlooking the Hudson River, feeling slightly disoriented and lost, she turned to Nick asleep beside her and felt settled. She was with him.

Nick wanted to give her all of Manhattan, but her requests were so simple. They visited the two main houses of worship on Fifth Avenue: St. Patrick's Cathedral and Bergdorf Goodman's. The cathedral was undergoing renovations and tangled in scaffolding. They slipped into an empty pew and stared in wonder at the ceiling and the innumerable arches all pointing heavenward. A peaceful silence amplified every footstep, every awkward cough. The air was heavy with incense, mass having let out just fifteen minutes earlier.

Nick draped an arm around Leila's shoulders and whispered, "I love the smell of incense."

"Are you Catholic?" she asked.

"I'm a capitalist," he replied. "Doesn't mean I can't appreciate top-shelf incense."

She bit her lip to suppress a laugh. "This really is the good stuff."

He nuzzled her ear. "The best."

Leila confessed she hadn't stepped foot in church since

her mother had died. Nick wasn't a praying man, but if he were he'd ask to feel this close to her forever.

The windows at Bergdorf's featured angelic mannequins with ostrich-feather wings. Nick practically had to drag her into the department store and up the escalator to the lingerie department. He insisted on buying her a gift and warned her it would be rude to say no.

Afterward, they went full-on tourist and toured Rockefeller Center. The day ended with a late meal. Burgers loaded with caramelized onions. Fries for her, rings for him.

Nick took her hand and licked ketchup off her fingertips. "What happens in January?"

She skirted the question. "Generally, you make resolutions you can't keep."

"You know what I'm talking about," he said.

"You mean what happens when you move here?"

He nodded.

"We move on. Rolling stones, remember?"

"Move on with other people?"

Leila looked nervous. She ran her palms on the red-and-white-checkered tablecloth. "That's how it works."

"There's one problem with that plan."

"Actually, it's pretty straightforward."

"I can't imagine you with someone else."

"I have the opposite problem. I can imagine you with any number of women."

"You're the only woman I want."

She kept her focus on her food, dipped a fry into a puddle of ketchup. "You'll be selling penthouses and brownstones in no time. You'll forget about me."

He pushed back his plate. "I want you to consider coming with me."

"Here? To Manhattan?"

"Yes."

"You can't be serious."

"I've never been more serious."

She closed her eyes. "Nick, is this trip about you getting me to follow you to New York?"

"It's about me wanting you in my life. You can't blame me for stacking the deck in my favor."

"You know real life isn't like a weekend getaway. Right?"

He leaned forward and lowered his voice. "Don't you like the idea even a little?"

"I like it a lot," she said. "Only let's not talk about it right now."

"Promise you'll give it serious thought."

"I promise."

Outside, darkness was falling. They were staying at the Standard, High Line in the Meatpacking District, which was a fixture in New York nightlife. When they got back to the room, Nick got a message from a friend asking to meet with him at the hotel bar. "He may be in the market for a condo in Brickell."

"What do you care?" Leila asked. "You're out of the Miami market."

"I'll co-list with Greg. He can take over when I'm gone."

"You can afford to take a break, Nick," Leila said. "If I were you, I'd be winding down."

"No, you wouldn't." He grabbed his wallet and keycard off the nightstand. "Give us one hour."

"No problem," she said. "The soaking tub is calling my name."

Nick hesitated to leave. Was it his imagination or was she relieved to see him gone? He knew he'd freaked her out with his request, but what choice did he have? Leaving her behind, living without her, wasn't an option for him.

Once Nick was gone, Leila was finally free to remove the corset of fear strapped around her waist and breathe deeply. She sat on the edge of the tub, waiting for it to fill. He'd made her promise to think about his offer, as if she could think about anything else.

Earlier at the Cathedral, she'd said a silent prayer asking to always feel as loved and cherished as she was at that moment. Her prayer must have been answered lightning fast because she had not anticipated Nick's proposal just hours later. Of course, she wanted to say yes. It would be no trouble at all to pack up her few things and follow him. He'd take care of everything, including her. She had no doubt his feelings for her were sincere. She had no doubt she loved him. But she knew stories that began with "I followed my boss/lover to a new city," generally did not end with "And we lived happily ever after."

Leila sank into the warm bath. From the tub she had a view of the city awakening for the night. This could be her future if she wanted it. But she had to be smart here. If she'd learned anything from Nick it was to stay focused. If things didn't work out between them, and what were the odds that they would, she'd be left with nothing. She'd agreed to eight weeks, no more. The only problem was telling Nick. How would he take rejection? She didn't want to find out anytime soon.

Miami welcomed them home with a damp hug, the triple assault of heat, humidity and the scent of rain in the air. They headed toward the long-term parking lot, wheeling their luggage behind them. Her car was on the fourth floor, his on the ground level. He followed her and helped load her luggage in the trunk.

"Are you coming home with me?" he asked.

"I shouldn't. I have to get organized for work tomorrow."

"I could stay at your place."

"Not ideal. I have a roommate and…"

He frowned. "I guess I can give you up for one night."

Her insides twisted with anxiety, not liking the idea of him giving her up at all. She wrapped her arms around his neck. "I'll never forget this weekend."

He smoothed her hair. "There'll be others."

Leila said nothing. Nick stiffened. "You've already made up your mind."

"No!" she cried unconvincingly. "Anyway, now isn't the time to get into it."

She tried to kiss his worries away, but he extracted himself from her arms.

"It's as good a time as any. Do you have something to tell me?"

Brick by brick, a wall was rising between them.

"I can't follow you to New York. Where will I work? What will I do?"

"You'll transfer with me. I already spoke to HR."

"Without even asking me?"

"The opportunity came up. They're looking to hire my assistant."

"And you said, 'Don't bother, my girlfriend is coming with me'?"

"That's not what I said, but if they want me, they don't have a choice."

"Do *I* have a choice?"

"Leila, tell me what you need and I'll make it happen."

A family of four walked past them pushing carts loaded with mismatched luggage. The parents eyed them with sympathy. They were just another volatile young couple having it out in a parking lot. Those days were surely long behind them.

"I'm going home," she said. "This is not one of your deals, Nick. You can't dictate the terms."

Chapter 14

Leila pulled out of the labyrinthine garage, tires screeching. His offer had all the trappings of a romantic gesture, but ultimately it was all lies. The last words they'd tossed at each other were still bouncing in her mind.

All you want is for me to be on hand for quick trips to the supply room.

You loved that. Don't act like you didn't.

I'm not trying to make a career out of it.

Leila, we're good together. What's wrong with trying to keep that?

Don't you see? You're only postponing the inevitable.

What's inevitable here?

Nothing. Forget it.

No matter how I play this, we're done. Is that right?

Raindrops were tapping on her windshield now. She switched on the wipers.

Put yourself in my shoes. Would you drop everything and follow a woman—your boss—to a new city?

What exactly are you dropping?

You entitled son of a —

She merged onto the highway and floored the pedal.

For Thanksgiving weekend, Nick went to visit his parents in Toronto. She spent the weekend in Naples with her aunt and caught up with old girlfriends.

Over lunch, they bragged about tedious but enviable internships or the complications of applying to grad school. Leila listened and offered encouragement, but had nothing to contribute. What could she possibly say? "I'm sleeping with my boss. He wants to promote me to professional girlfriend, but I'm still thinking about it." She returned to Miami, her pride bruised but her resolve hardened.

* * *

Nick hadn't softened, either. Determined to smooth things over, he apologized with flowers and a card reading, "Yes, I'm an entitled SOB, but I'm truly sorry." He apologized with a gift of La Perla lingerie. A tulle-and-lace bodysuit that must have cost as much as her rent—but not as much as her purse. He apologized in person, waiting until the office emptied out before timidly approaching her desk. She pretended to be in a hurry, packing up her things with unnecessary concentration and focus.

"Leila, look at me."

She exhaled forcefully but complied because, more than anything, she needed this to end. She needed to be with him. The nights spent alone were agony. Still, she took her time, putting her purse aside and switching off her phone. When she raised her eyes, she was stunned by how adorable he looked. He had a boyish expression of contrition, at once humble and fearful, that tugged at her heart.

"I hate that you're okay with my leaving."

"I'm not okay with it. I hate it, but it *is* happening."

"You've been so damn casual about."

Now they'd come to something. It was time to come clean.

"You're right about me," she said. "I don't have much going on. But before I met you I had goals, a plan. Now all I do is follow you around. I *can't* follow you to New York. I have to work on me."

"Leila, we make a good team."

She wasn't so sure. It was a team in which she had absolutely no leverage. He'd consult her, but his decisions would be final. What kind of team was that?

"I don't know enough to be on your team," she said. "We're not at the same level. All I'd do is defer to you."

Nick looked away. He was losing the argument and, she could tell, his patience.

"Hey, we can stay in touch."

"That's crap and you know it. How long before men start coming after you?"

Leila scoffed. "Is that all you're worried about?"

"Hell, yes, I'm worried about it."

"Nick, we still have time," she reminded him. "And I don't want to waste it fighting."

But that was exactly what they did.

Any petty disagreement spiraled into a full-blown argument. Afterward, they'd put away the knives and make up in bed. He'd kiss her in unusual places—her collarbone, her hips—and apologize for whatever insensitive thing he'd said. She'd admit to having started the fight in the first place. On and on they went, circling the opening of a black hole.

Chapter 15

Nick hadn't planned on attending the party—a broker's open at a Coconut Grove estate that he, on his way out, was no longer in any position to consider seriously. He'd ignored the invitation, but saw it now as an opportunity for him and Leila to break the pattern they'd fallen into. Too many fights. For once, he had no interest in make-up sex. He wanted to hear her laugh, to see her eyes light up with curiosity. This event was perfect, not too obvious. They attended brokers' open houses all the time. Granted, this one was rather extraordinary.

He waited for her out front, hanging out and talking basketball with the valet attendants. "Aren't you coming in?" he was asked more than once when friends arrived. "In a minute." He didn't want Leila to venture alone into a house full of strangers. He'd noticed how shy she was at their first open house, uncomfortable in the crowd. He felt protective of her.

When she pulled up in the little red convertible, he was glad that he'd waited. The boys at the valet tripped over each other to get to her. He watched from the top of the steps, amused, until she stepped out in red lace with straps so fine they were practically invisible to the naked eye.

He stepped forward and chased the pack of wolves away.

"Leila, my God."

He was speechless. Earlier he'd asked her to wear the red dress from their first open house, the one that tied with a knot.

"The other dress was at the cleaner's," she said.

He pulled her close. "You're so good to me."

She laughed, and he knew that they were going to have a good night. He led her by the hand through an arched portico. She looked up and took in the sprawling two-story Mediterranean estate. "What do we have here?"

He loved that she was as excited as he was. He squeezed her hand. "Let's find out."

In the foyer, Leila gasped at the limestone floors and high, vaulted ceiling. "This is amazing!" In the game room, they played a round of pool. She sucked at it, but it gave him the opportunity to lean over her, touch her and watch her attempt impossible shots from every angle. After a while, he yanked the cue stick out of her hands. It was giving him ideas. In the meditation room, she tried to get him to sit still and clear his mind. He stormed out. They headed up the staircase and wandered through the eight bedrooms. In the panic room or sex dungeon—who were they kidding?—he pinned her to the leather-upholstered wall.

"What are you doing?" she asked.

"You wore this dress to seduce me," he said. "Here I am, seduced."

Touching a finger to her chin, he drew her in for a kiss. She pulled back. "Did you at least lock the door?"

She had to know him better than that. "Come on, Leila."

Twenty minutes later, outside by the pool, she stood close to him, seeking warmth. True to her nature, she asked, "How much are they asking for this place?"

"No idea." For once he didn't care. He wrapped his arms around her waist and tugged her to him. But she stiffened and pulled away.

"Greg is here. Look to your left."

He didn't bother. "And?"

"He can't see us together."

"Leila, I'm not hiding from Greg."

He didn't care about the optics. Being here with her felt natural.

"We're not hiding," she said, moving further away. "We're playing it safe."

"Where are you going?"

She pointed to the house. "Ladies' room."

Nick watched her as she briskly walked away. If he was fated to fall hard for a woman someday, that day had come.

As time raced on, they kept to themselves, enjoying each other's company and avoiding crowds. However, they couldn't avoid attending the office holiday party. For the occasion, Leila purchased a deep blue dress with a plunging V neckline. The look was over-the-top for an office event, but she didn't care. She was competing with the imaginary New York fashionistas lining up to replace her in Nick's life.

The party was held at the Clevelander. A fixture of South Beach, the hotel's open-air patio offered views of the Atlantic. Nick was waiting at one of the bars. She'd insisted they show up and leave separately, for appearances' sake. The look on his face validated the effort she'd put into her outfit, not to mention the expense. However, once they joined the party they were ripped apart. Nick was the man of the hour, the holiday party doubling as his send-off under the banner New York Nick. He was congratulated, celebrated and, at one point, surrounded by dancers in Vegas-worthy show gear.

After an hour, Leila stepped to the terrace edge. Some guests, mostly clients, were huddled together, smoking. Craving pure salt air, she fled the party. She rode the private elevator to the ground floor and crossed Ocean Drive, leaving the neon hustle and bustle behind for the beach. Her heels dug into the rough sand. She kicked them off and cradled them in her arms.

The beach was quiet. The rolling waves echoed the worries of her heart. Was she making a mistake, letting him go? How many men like Nick were there out there? She quickly reminded herself that this wasn't about Nick or any man. This was about her, putting focus and energy on her, rather than him.

Her phone rang. Without hesitation, she took it to her ear and said, "I'm out for a walk."

"In the dark?" Nick asked.

"Needed some air, that's all. Are you done with your farewell tour?"

"Leila, I have to play the game."

"I'm only asking if you're done."

"All done," he said. "Now I'm all yours."

"Good." She closed her eyes. The night breeze was cool on her skin. "I need you to make love to me."

A pause suggested that he took her request seriously. "All you ever have to do is ask."

Leila drove with the car radio off. When she pulled onto the Venetian, the causeway unfolded ahead lined by romantic lampposts. She lowered the car windows and breathed deeply. Nick had enlisted Greg to sell his place. She would not be making this trip again.

She let herself in with her key and waited for him on the balcony. When she heard him at the door, her breath grew shallow.

Nick called out, "Where are you?"

She didn't respond. She waited for him to find her, which he did easily. The sliding-glass door squeaked open and he stood in the doorway.

"I should've known."

She turned away and kept her eyes on the water's surface. Her tears were near.

"Are you still mad?" he asked.

Mad was far less complicated than *sad*, so she went with that. It was sad to hear him say goodbye and to feel beforehand the vacuum of his absence. And sad was the slight change in attitude she'd noticed these last few days. They fought less, mainly because he'd stopped taking the bait. He'd given up on her.

Nick approached, gathered her hair out of his way and kissed her neck. "Remember that first morning when I found you out here?"

"Of course, I remember."

"You were wearing next to nothing. You looked incredible in the sun."

Nick's hands roamed her body. He tested the deep V of her neckline, finding it allowed easy access. She tried to turn around and he stopped her.

"Hold on to the rail."

"What if—?"

"Someone sees us?" He leaned against her, offering concrete proof that he was beyond caring. He said, "I need this, too."

Leila closed her eyes, but could still see the twinkle of the distant city lights. Modesty was a virtue for the suburbs.

The agency shut down from Christmas Eve through New Year's Day. Leila was relieved that they could drop the act and finally just be. Christmas was celebrated with a tabletop tree and Chinese takeout. On New Year's Day, she insisted on making squash soup as per her dad's family tradition.

"For breakfast?" Nick asked.

"It's tradition!"

They'd ushered in the New Year with a midnight boat ride and fireworks over the bay. Although she was tired and not at all sure she had all the ingredients, she insisted on making the recipe. Despite her best efforts, the soup turned out like paste. Despondent, Leila shoveled the thick mass into the trash. She'd wanted to share something personal about herself before… Frankly, before it was too late. She'd botched it.

"Want to try my family tradition of mac and cheese?" Nick teased.

"No."

"Want me to pick up coffee and bagels at the deli?"

"Yes, please."

He hugged her. "I love that you tried."

The next day at dawn she drove him to the airport. Traffic was thin; they arrived at MIA in record speed. Nick declined her offer to park and walk with him to the departure gait.

"It's so early. We could get coffee."

"I'd rather not."

He was dressed for another climate in a black sweater and dark jeans. Leila gripped the steering wheel with both hands. A SUV pulled up to the curb just ahead and a young couple jumped out, hugging, kissing, saying goodbye like normal people.

"Fine. Let's do it your way."

"We're doing this your way. Remember?"

"Don't start."

If he was so eager to go, she wished he'd get out of her car, get this whole thing over with.

"When did you fall in love with me?" Nick asked.

"What? I never said—"

"Want me to go first?"

Leila looked straight ahead. If she flinched or even blinked, she'd come unhinged.

"The second I laid eyes on you, Leila," he said. "I had to pick a fight with Jo-Ann to hold it together. It was that quick. Now you tell me."

Leila's grip on the wheel loosened and her hands fell onto her lap. "I heard your voice through the door."

Before she'd ever laid eyes on him, she'd heard him on the phone, flirting, laughing—quintessential Nick Adrian. His voice, rich and nuanced, had grabbed her by the throat, demanding that she pay attention.

"You told me that you have a habit of putting stock in the wrong things."

"For once that's not what I'm doing," she said. "This is the *opposite* of that."

"Are you sure?" Nick reached for the door handle. "You think you'll move on with some nice guy, some idiot who doesn't know you, all the things you like. Think you'll be happy? Go ahead and try."

What about happiness?

Leila sat in her car in the office building's garage, turning the question over in her mind. Nick's last words had stung. She'd made the smart decision, but why did she feel so dumb? What about happiness? The joy of seeing Nick in the morning, spending the day with him, working beside him, undressing for him at night… She couldn't put it on her résumé, but it mattered. Now she'd have to do without it. She willed herself to cry, hoping for some relief. But the sickening feeling in her gut wasn't sorrow, it was regret. She was certain now. She'd made a mistake.

Leila climbed out of the car and leaned against it, feeling a numbing tingle in her legs. What could she do now? Make a mad dash to the airport like in the movies? She had no choice but to move forward.

She rode up to the office. It was early and the reception desk was deserted. She slowly made her way down the hall toward her desk. To make it through the morning, and what promised to be a tough day, she'd need a lot of coffee. She'd forgotten to brew some and Nick wasn't going to show up with Starbucks. She couldn't wait for the 2:00 p.m. *cafecito* break. She was on her own. That simple realization was all it took. Tears washed down her face. She leaned against a wall and let out one unmistakable sob.

"Are you all right?"

Oh, God, not now.

Jo-Ann was waiting for her at her desk, holding a huge cardboard box, the framed photograph of Leila and her aunt peeking out from above the rim. Leila quickly wiped her eyes under Jo-Ann's cool gaze. Her expression was unmistakable. *I sure as hell told you so.* And, yes, she had.

PART TWO

Chapter 16

One year later

Leila had not—*not at all*—set out to be the girl who had sex with an ex two seconds after saying hello, but that's exactly the girl she turned out to be. The early rush of tenderness had washed away quickly. Nick was hard; he met the demands of her body. As he dove into her, the shell-lined wall scraped her back. He silenced her cries with hot, hostile kisses. Something was coming loose inside her. How could she have gone so long without this?

They'd achieved the right amount of push and pull, perfect balance, when he asked for more. "Leila, say it. I need to hear it."

"Oh, God, Nick…"

"Come on, Leila," he said, speaking softly against her parted lips even as his grip tightened. "Tell me, sweetheart…tell me, love…"

"Nick…" She cupped his face. "Shut up."

She knew what he wanted to hear, and she wasn't going to say it.

He kissed her again, hard. "Say you love me. Say it."

"I love you. Damn it!"

Nick drove deeper inside her. Suddenly her skies lit up with stars. Leila cried, tipping backward, on a slow fall back to earth, back to him.

He held her close, his breath in shreds, coming down from his own high. But when he spoke, his voice was steady. "Don't forget it."

To hell with this man!

Leila pushed him away, wriggled her skirt down over her hips and found a lost shoe. The party music and noises drifted in, reminding her of where she was and how far off course she'd drifted. All the while, Nick whistled as he buttoned his shirt. "Now would be a good time to visit that cigar-rolling station."

She brushed her hair off her face and glared at him. She loved him less already.

"What's the problem, sweetheart?"

What's the problem...sweetheart? Leila turned and *flew* out of the cave.

"Hey, wait!" Nick cried, going after her.

"Leave me alone!"

She stomped up the wide stone steps, entered the house through the loggia, got lost in the maze of rooms and ended up outside again, on a terrace that descended into the bay. A handful of couples enjoyed the astonishing view. A stone barge rose out of the water just a few feet off shore, a magnificent ghost ship. Astonished, Leila couldn't tear her eyes off it. Her moment of hesitation allowed Nick to catch up to her. He gripped her by the arm. She tensed and pulled away, but something fleeting in his eyes stopped her heart.

Before she could say anything, a woman's voice cut in. "There you are!"

It was Paige Conner from Raul Reyes's inner circle. She was decidedly friendlier this time around. Leila said hello before realizing Paige was speaking to Nick.

"Are you having a good time?" Paige asked him.

"I'm having a blast," Nick said dryly.

"Awesome." Turning to Leila, she said, "Hey, I lost your card but now that you've met our new sales director, it's all good. Right?"

Nick shook his head. "That's how rumors get started, Paige."

"Don't worry. The old man will hire you. I have a good feeling."

Leila studied Nick, the new sales director of Reyes Realty. True or not, it made sense to her that his star would keep rising while she was left flailing in the dust.

Picking up on the tension, Paige excused herself. "Have a good night."

Leila straightened to gain some height. "You're working for Reyes now?"

"He hasn't made an offer," Nick said. "But I'm looking for a reason to say yes if he does."

A double shot of anger and envy struck her full-on. "Well, keep looking."

By some miracle, she managed to find her way out of the fun house and back to her car. She drove with the top down, her hair slapping her face. When a bunch of guys pulled up next to her at a light, she responded to the catcalls with a finger. She was not herself. At any minute she could snap.

She arrived at the rented bungalow on Alton North that she called home and also office. The Miami Beach location kept her in the market she had hoped to crack into, but it was far from ideal. Tucked under an overpass, her bedroom often reeked of gas exhaust. The city was installing hydro pumps to control floodwater; she and her neighbors were cut off from the main road by all the construction mess. She often felt walled in by noise, car engines and jackhammers. But it made for the most affordable rent around.

Leila parked in the back alley and let herself in through the front door. What once was a living room was now her reception area with a desk and a couple of chairs. Her office was a converted second bedroom. The kitchen/break room was in its original state with Formica cabinets, a chipped tile counter and a yellowing vinyl floor. The Florida International University coffee mug in the shallow sink belonged to her assistant, Brie. The one bathroom was off to the right, turquoise tile and brass fixtures. Down a short and narrow hall was her private space, the former master bedroom turned one-room apartment.

Leila kicked off her heels and fell into her unmade bed. She was exhausted. Her rage had dissipated on the drive home, leaving her with the earthy scent of the grotto, Nick's touch, his kiss and her name turned into a soulful mantra. He'd asked what had changed. She rested a hand on her heart and felt its steady beating. *Nothing's changed.*

Chapter 17

Nick's decision to return to Miami was irrational and impulsive. Two things he wasn't. The catalyst was a girl with pink hair.

He was in a Greenwich Village tavern wrapping up a meeting with a couple looking to sell their three-story brownstone. He stepped up to the bar to settle the tab when he spotted a young woman shying away from him, hiding her face with the longer strands of her pink bob.

"Kim," he called out. "Is that you?"

She groaned.

Undeterred, Nick joined her, sliding onto a free bar stool, dropping his phone and keys onto the bar. "Why would you hide from me? I thought we were buddies."

Kim drummed the smooth mahogany bar top with her lacquered fingernails. "What girl in her right mind wouldn't hide from her boss on a Friday night?"

"Fair point. But what are you doing *here*?" The classic pub was too fussy for a cool girl like Kim. Her baby-pink hair and emerald-green fingernails were in sharp contrast with the Tiffany lamps and high-polished wood surfaces.

She gave him a long, hard look. "Getting stood up, that's what."

"Oh, come on!" Nick cried, outraged. "What are we drinking?"

"Could I have a shot of tequila?" Oddly, she sounded like a child shyly asking for an ice cream cone.

"You could, but why would you?" Nick ordered two vodka martinis, hers was strawberry-flavored. "If and when he gets here, he shouldn't catch you drowning your sorrows in tequila. Not a hot look."

Kim thanked him. "Good thinking."

Nick waited until their drinks were served before asking, "Who's the jerk?"

She swirled the rosy liquid in her glass. "Ethan Harper. Total dweeb."

"Do the kids still say 'dweeb'?"

She pointed to his phone. "Google him."

Nick indulged his young assistant. Several images of a skinny guy with a crooked smile popped up. Ethan Harper was an actor who performed regularly on Broadway—as an extra.

"He's a waiter at the steakhouse across the street," Kim said.

Nick tapped on one photo, pinched it and glanced at Kim. "He's a kid."

"Hey!" she cried. "We can't all date studs like you."

That made Nick smile. He whispered conspiringly, "Is that what people think? That I'm a stud?"

"Please! You can have any woman at the agency and some of the guys, too. Just say the word and I'll hook you up."

"Way to pimp me out, Kim," Nick said. "How about you focus on updating my sales figures?"

"I saw you working your magic over there. Did you sign that couple?"

"Of course."

"Is there anything you can't do?"

"I can't let a pretty girl sit alone at a bar."

Kim relaxed. "This is nice, I guess, getting to know each other outside the office."

Over the past months they'd developed a good rapport. She was competent and kept him organized. They'd never discussed their private lives. He'd drawn lines and never crossed them.

"Permission to speak freely, sir?"

"Permission granted."

"Are you sleeping with that broker, Christine?"

"What the hell?"

Yeah, sure he was. But to be questioned about it was surprising.

"She calls the office a lot. I'm sure she has your cell number, so she's only calling *me* to check up on *you*. Doesn't she work?"

"Christine works." In fact, she was one of New York's top brokers. That's how they'd met, after all. Although, she was always available and up for anything he had in mind, no questions asked.

"I'll tell her not to call the office anymore."

Kim joined her hands in prayer. "Thank you, Lord!"

It was a chilly September evening and she looked stylish in a black sweater and black boots that reached her thighs. Ethan Harper didn't know what he was missing. Nick nudged her in the ribs. "See? We make a great team."

Kim nearly spit out her strawberry-flavored martini. "We're not a team. You're the boss and I'm the girl who says, 'Yes, boss.'"

"That's bull. I value your opinion."

"When have you ever asked for my opinion?"

Her complaints sounded familiar and made him uncomfortable. "Am I that big of a jerk?"

"Do I still have permission—?"

"Yeah. Talk."

"You're a one-man show. You call the shots—and that's very hot. But you're no team player."

Nick didn't know what to make of this. There was some fundamental flaw in his character. Whatever gene turned benevolent rulers into despots, he apparently had it. This was odd, considering he was, after all, a mild-mannered Canadian, born and raised in Toronto. Maybe his attitude was shaped by the business. He'd figured early that every man and woman were out for themselves. And he'd adjusted, maybe too well.

"I didn't mean to upset you," Kim said quietly. "You're a great boss."

He reassured her. "It's nothing I haven't heard before."

"May I ask one more question?"

"Go ahead."

"Did some chick break your heart?"

Nick swiveled in his seat. She was full of surprises tonight. "Where did that come from?"

"You may look like you have it going on and all, but sometimes you look sad."

All the women on the dating wheel, including Christine, had complained he seemed distracted, accusing him of being too absorbed with work. Only Kim had broached the truth, confirming an old theory of his: the women he worked with knew him best.

Had some "chick" broken his heart? No. Broken hearts were for teenagers in love. One woman—Leila—had ripped his heart out of his chest and hurled it off a cliff.

"Want to talk about it?"

"No."

Just then Nick spotted Ethan Harper timidly making his way toward them. The guy wore a black puffer jacket and gray skinny jeans. He and Kim would get along fine. Nick leaned closer to Kim and whispered, "Laugh like I said something hysterical."

Kim took the cue and ran with it, letting out a flirtatious little giggle. "Oh, you're so crazy!"

The flustered young man tapped Kim on the shoulder and, beanie hat in hand, apologized for keeping her waiting.

Ain't love grand? Nick thought, watching them shuffle out of the pub. Then a crazy idea swirled in his mind, gathering speed and momentum. He picked up his phone and typed another name into the search engine. Leila Amis.

Waiting for the results to pop up, his heart hammered

against his ribs. The last time he'd Googled her, searching for her old pageant pictures, he'd gotten into trouble. He hadn't done it since. The search results today were quite different from the past: a website—LeilaAmisRealty.com—a Twitter account and an Instagram page.

He tapped on the Instagram link and scrolled through post after post of shots of Leila at cocktail parties, at charity luncheons or posing prettily next to Sold signs, although not very many. She wore her long black hair straight and dressed more conservatively than he liked, but damn it if she wasn't more beautiful than before. Her mocha skin was so rich he could lick the screen. Nick studied each picture, a ball of pain forming in his gut. Leila looking happy, confident and free—looking like her life had gotten a hell of a lot better without him in it.

That didn't sit well with him.

It hadn't taken much. He'd put out a few feelers. Within weeks he was on a plane to Miami to meet with Raul Reyes, one of the world's wealthiest people, according to all the business magazines. The word was Reyes was looking for someone new, fresh and eager to lead the sales of his luxury condo building on Biscayne. Nick was scheduled to meet with him at his office for an overview of the project and, later in the evening, he would attend his book launch party. Nick couldn't wait to hear about the new building, the book though was bull.

Cruising from the airport in the back of a cab, Nick welcomed the assault of bright, tropical color. Miami was the city he loved but for some reason couldn't manage to plant lasting roots. The things he cherished had a way of slipping through his fingers. His new goal was to change that trend.

Nick switched on his phone. Immediately it started to chime and flash text messages, missed calls and voice mails. And then it started to ring. Christine. He hit Ignore, but ignoring her wasn't as easy as that. They'd done a few good deals together and he never liked to cut off a business contact, no matter how messy things got between them.

When the phone rang again, he answered. "I'm traveling."

"To Miami. For a job interview."

"Who told you?"

"So it's true! What are you thinking, Nick? Who trades Manhattan for Miami before retirement?"

His boss, Connie Madison, had had the same reaction when he'd told her. But they didn't know this city like he did. This sales position would be the perfect way to reenter the market.

"Hey, thanks for the career advice."

"What about us?" Christine asked. "We were good together."

"Christine," he said softly, "there is no 'us.'"

"Don't say that."

Nick closed his eyes. He'd been saying it for two weeks now. When would she hear him?

"I don't know what else to say."

"You're going to regret this move," she said. "The Miami market crashes every ten years or so. And the women are tacky and dumb."

Nick couldn't hold back a laugh. Overconfidence. They had that in common. "I'm going to miss you."

"Oh, go to hell!"

The line went dead and Nick pocketed his phone. The driver peered at him in the rearview mirror. "How did I do?" Nick asked through the open partition.

The driver nodded. "Sometimes you have to lay it down."

Nick leaned back and stared out the window. *Miami women are tacky and dumb.* Not true. But he didn't care about the city's female population in general. He cared about Leila. Finding her. Getting her back.

Their split had revealed that she was capable of cruelty. He'd thought her perfect. He'd thought her all love and sweetness. He'd been afraid of hurting *her,* and had never thought to protect himself. When it was all said and done, she had broken his heart. And yet he wanted her back.

Now only twenty-fours after landing in Miami, Nick was sure he'd made the right decision. The meeting with Reyes had gone well. And meeting Leila at the party was a clear sign. It had whetted his appetite.

Chapter 18

The morning after the party, Leila was at her desk, determined to put Nick out of her mind. The lucky bastard was considering yet another promotion. Well, congrats to him! She had to hustle to make things happen.

Leila reviewed her calendar and called her assistant into her office. "Brie, I'm meeting with the newlyweds in Homestead today. Is there anything else on the horizon?"

Brie switched on her personal iPad and scrolled through email. "You *may* have a property appraisal in the Grove around four. But nothing's confirmed."

Leila perked up. "That sounds promising."

"It isn't," Brie said. "I'm talking about the bad side of the Grove, like right on the tracks."

"Doesn't matter," she said. "I'll take anything. I'm not picky. Not anymore. Anything else?"

"George Miller called," Brie said. "He's heading home to Atlanta for a couple of weeks. He wants to meet for lunch when he gets back."

Leila winced. When she'd first signed Miller, she'd celebrated with champagne. The lawyer was officially her first big-money client. And he was searching for a house in the heart of Coral Gables to relocate his family. But he'd balked at every single property she'd showed him. She was beginning to think he wasn't serious.

Brie settled in a chair across from Leila's desk, in no apparent hurry to get to work. "You look a little tired this morning."

Leila swallowed the impulse to reach for a compact mirror. "I need a massage."

"May I say something crazy?" Brie asked.

"Like I can stop you."

"A massage isn't going to cut it. You need to let off some

steam." Brie rattled off some suggestions. "Call your girls, get out there, go dancing…"

"Is that your expert advice?"

Leila glanced at Brie—@QueenBrie_21, 10K followers—taking in her flawless brown skin, curly afro and artful nails. Nineteen, full-time college student, part-time office assistant, blogger. Brie reminded her what it meant to be free, creative and confident. Leila was only six years older, but she felt ancient in her beige pantsuit. She'd ordered it online with no concern about the cut or the fit because that's how little she cared for beige pantsuits.

"Not really," Brie replied. "I'd tell you to get laid, but that would be crossing the line."

Brie couldn't point out the fine line of discretion with night-vision goggles.

Leila got up and grabbed her keys and her purse. "I'm off to meet the newlyweds. Confirm lunch with Miller. Any day he wants."

Brie made a face. "Can't stand that guy. He rubs me the wrong way."

"Join the club."

"I want a decent second bedroom for a nursery, not a shoebox! Why is that too much to ask?"

Leila's newlywed clients were in the midst of an emotional windstorm. After touring two town homes in neighboring gated communities, the wife broke down, heartbroken over the limitations of their capped budget. Meanwhile her husband paced the floor and mumbled the dreaded words, "Let's just rent a place."

Goodbye sales commission.

Leila stepped out onto the porch to give them some privacy. She checked her text messages.

From Brie: Coconut Grove canceled.

From Sofia, who'd gotten her into Reyes's party: Let's meet for drinks.

She responded to her friend's message. Sure. When? Where?

Sofia's reply: Tobacco Road. I'm free at five.

Leila sighed. She was pretty much free all day.

Tobacco Road was a bona fide dive in the heart of Brickell. Leila knew why Sofia had picked it. With the neighborhood's wild development, the century-old bar would be closing soon. Still, having to return to Brickell was bittersweet for Leila. From the sidewalk outside the bar, she could see the top of the building where she and Nick once worked.

Sofia Silva was waiting at the upstairs lounge. She looked fresh and smart in a white blazer and pencil skirt. The bright color flattered her cinnamon-brown skin. Her reddish brown hair fell to her shoulders in disheveled waves. She and Sofia had reconnected a few months ago at a Businesswomen of Greater Miami luncheon, and discovered they had a lot in common, both working to establish footing in their respective fields. Sometime between the appetizer and entrée, and fifteen minutes into the keynote speaker's speech, Sofia had leaned over and whispered, "I hate these self-important bitches." With those words, an alliance was forged. They'd started their own private chapter of Miami businesswomen. It was Sofia who'd recommended Leila scrap her marketing plan based on pricey sidewalk bench ads. "Use social media instead," she'd said.

Sofia greeted Leila with typical bluntness. "You don't look so hot."

"It's been a long day."

"Sit down. I want to hear all about last night's party, all the juicy details."

Leila opened a menu. "Why juicy? Nothing *juicy* happened." She was trying hard not to sound paranoid. "I didn't get to talk with Reyes, if that's what you're asking."

"Well, I'm not." Sofia snapped a picture of her cocktail, a bourbon concoction that harkened to the bar's speakeasy days, and posted it on Instagram before holding out her phone. "I'm asking about Nick Adrian."

Leila stared at a picture of her and Nick descending the grand stairs toward the Vizcaya gardens, hand in hand. She noticed details that had escaped her last night, like the cut of his suit and the newly defined angle of his chin. The look in his eyes was determined but grim. She was grateful her hair had concealed her face.

All day she'd forced Nick out of her mind. And now here he was in glorious high-definition.

"Who posted that?"

"Some blog. Read the caption."

Leila sighed. "'Nicolas Adrian and sexy companion.'"

"Of course, they know his name." Wasn't the objective of last night's outing to get *her* name out there?

"I can get the blogger to edit the caption. He's a friend."

"Don't bother." She could just imagine the new caption: Leila Amis, Formerly Known as Nicolas Adrian's Sexy Companion.

Sofia hammered her with questions. "What's going on here? And when did Nick get back in town?"

"I don't know. I ran into him at the party."

"That's it? That's all you're going to say?"

"It's a long story and I don't want to get into it."

"You're getting into it, whether you want to or not," Sofia said. "I deserve this information."

Leila grabbed Sofia's glass and took a gulp. There really was no escaping Nick.

Sofia flagged the waiter and ordered a second cocktail. Then she ordered Leila to talk.

"It's what it looks like," Leila said finally.

"I always had a feeling about you two." Sofia held up her phone again, displaying the incriminating evidence. "But this looks serious. Do you see the look in the man's eyes? He's not playing around."

Leila rested her chin on her palm. She was near tears. "No, he wasn't."

"All this time you've been hiding this hot secret. This makes me love you so much more!"

"You don't get it," Leila said. "It was a mistake, and I *paid* for it."

"You always do," Sofia said. "Especially when you work together."

"I was his assistant. I worked *for* him."

"Well, skip to the part when you met your hot boss and wanted to hop on his desk."

"It wasn't like that," Leila said. "Well, it was, but it wasn't."

"Oh, God. You fell in love."

Leila nodded.

"Sloppy love?"

She nodded again. That was a good way to describe it.

"And?"

"You know. He moved to New York City for a promotion."

"Isn't that how it goes?" Sofia mused. "The good ones always packing and leaving for NYC? Then moving back after a few harsh winters."

The waiter arrived with her drink. Leila stared at it.

"He wants you back," Sofia said.

"I don't know what he wants."

From the taste of things, revenge was more like it.

Sofia clapped with joy. "*Love* it."

Chapter 19

Since opening her agency, Leila had relied on the Nicolas Adrian real-estate playbook, charging pricey lunches and dinners to woo, or in this case, retain clients.

George Miller, her client from hell, had picked Versailles, a popular Cuban restaurant with a French name. She'd arrived early and sat waiting a full half-hour. The waiter refilled her water glass time and again. He suggested, in Spanish, that she order an appetizer. When she declined, the look he gave her required no interpretation. This wasn't a coffee shop where she could hang out and daydream and not run a tab. This was Versailles at the peak of lunch hour. The table she was holding was prime real estate.

Her table offered a full view of the restaurant floor. This was her first visit to the famous establishment, better known as a political hotspot than a culinary destination. But then, Miller was new to Miami and likely still picking venues off the internet. These days the patrons of Versailles were more likely to plot business mergers rather than regime change. She imagined business transactions concluding in the time it took to brew a *cortadito*. As she watched, she grew hungry and her hunger fed her frustration.

Finally, Miller arrived. He stormed past the poor hostess who was struggling to do her job and lead the way. His eyes were hidden behind mirrored Ray-Bans. He strode up to the table, hovering silently over her for a few seconds, and something inside her shrank. Evidently her clients weren't the charming and delightful people that Nick had the privilege of wining and dining.

He took a seat and spread the cloth napkin on his lap. "I'm not going to renew our contract when it expires. I'll tell you that right now."

If she didn't deliver, he would drop her.

Leila took the punch to her gut but did not waver. She looked across the table at him with a smile pasted on her face.

He followed up with a second blow. "I knew you were inexperienced. Thought I'd give you a chance, anyway. But if it turns out you wasted my time, I'll put it out there. I'm not kidding."

Alarmed, Leila tried to defend herself. "I've showed you every single property in your price range and you've hated every one of them."

"I want 'wow.'"

"You don't have a 'wow' budget."

It was time for real talk. Her reputation was on the line.

"Those houses were overpriced," he said. "You know it."

"We've been through this. The market sets the price. Not me. Not you."

"Your *job* is to drive the price down. That's why I hired you."

"Look, I have a couple of listings lined up. One is in the Gables. It's been on the market for a while now. The price was slashed twenty percent yesterday, which puts it in your range. And it meets most of your requirements."

Miller's wife and kids were back in Atlanta, waiting out the school year. This gave him some time to waste. In the meantime his firm had put him up in a condo on Ponce de Leon, and he was enjoying the quasi-single life. His list of wants and needs was pretty straightforward. A stellar school district was a must. His wife had requested an up-dated kitchen and the kids wanted a yard large enough to accommodate the dog Miller had promised to sweeten the prospect of moving to a new state.

"Why has it been sitting on the market for so long?" he asked.

"It needs cosmetic work."

The listing agent had described the old house as "charming," which was never good. But a fixer in the Gables was well worth the trouble. The City Beautiful, as they called it, was the place to plant roots if you wanted to join Miami's tightest social circles. Miller and his wife would have access to the Women's Club, Junior League, shopping, theater and the Biltmore golf course. A renovation was a small price to pay. After all, a diamond was a diamond even when covered with crap.

"The second property?"

"It's in South Miami."

"Damn it! I said—"

"I know what you said. What's the harm in looking?"

Miller ordered calamari for the table. "My schedule is tight today. How about we see this first property and check out the other tomorrow around noon?"

How about we skip calamari and get started now? Leila was smart enough to bite those words. She wasn't exactly standing on solid ground.

"Sounds like a plan."

A while later, Miller followed her down US-1 toward Coral Gables. They sped along winding roads and through canopies of mature oaks, around a series of roundabouts leading to a dead-end street bordered by a canal. They pulled up to a two-story Mediterranean Revival with a For Sale sign planted in the front yard.

Leila got out of her car, the same red Miata she'd had for years now, and took a minute to study the house before Miller tainted her judgment. Unfortunately she hadn't had a chance to preview it and the tight-angled photographs she'd studied hadn't revealed much.

The house was an Old-Spanish charmer, a coveted Miami classic, and despite its yellowed stucco façade, chipped barrel-tile roof and overgrown lawn dotted with bright yellow dandelions, it was worth something. Built in 1921, it had been gutted and renovated in 1991, which was a great big red flag. Nineties-era renovations were the absolute worst.

Miller took out his phone and snapped a picture "for

the missus." He turned to her and said, "Not much curb appeal, huh?"

She asked him to keep an open mind.

They walked up a cracked stone path that doubled as a bed for intrepid weeds. The medieval front door was studded with iron nails. Leila had the combination to the lockbox. After a struggle, the door creaked open. Before letting Miller in, she turned to him and said, "This could be a great deal. The owner is eighty-five and lived here alone until she fell down the stairs and broke her hip. Needless to say, she's a motivated seller."

They entered a tight foyer that presented all the signs of an identity crisis: a tray ceiling with an iron candelabra above and a groovy shaggy carpet below.

Miller sighed. "Good grief."

They walked through the first floor, inspecting the closed-in kitchen with mismatched appliances and the dining room with frosted-mirror paneling. In the living room, Leila announced that they'd reached the heart of the house and pointed out the ceiling lined with hand-painted cypress beams, a masterpiece of craftsmanship. The ceiling's appeal was undermined by a botched faux-finish paint job that stripped the room of any authentic mid-twenties appeal.

They climbed the grand staircase that had sealed the owner's fate. Leila thought the master bedroom lovely, but Miller frowned at the pink-and-green floral wallpaper. She threw open the French doors and stepped out onto a generous Juliet balcony overlooking a courtyard littered with brittle palm fronds. The sultry afternoon heat caused her skin to bead with sweat.

"What do you think?" she asked.

"It's a disaster."

"You've got to be kidding!" She'd blurted out the words and immediately wanted to recall them. Real Estate 101: the client's tastes were not to be questioned.

"Don't get me wrong," Miller said. "It's not a bad house. If my grandma were looking for a place, this would be it."

She gently proposed they leave his grandmother out of it and consider the property's potential. Whether he knew it or not, this house was perfect for him. "Think of your boys. They'd be so happy here. This is the right house on the right street in an excellent school district. Yes, it needs TLC—"

"SOS is more like it."

"It's nothing a little money and a savvy decorator can't fix. This house has great bones. And the price is bargain basement for the area. If you don't grab it today, someone else will."

"Let them have it," Miller said gruffly. "It's not for me."

She shut the balcony doors, snuffing out the street noise. The matter was settled. "Maybe we'll have better luck tomorrow."

"Doubt it."

Sidewalk access to the agency was obstructed by construction debris, large piles of chewed-up concrete and gravel made pretty by a ring of bright orange cones. The city had put up signs reminding drivers that the barricaded shops were in fact open for business and remote parking was available somewhere. They only had to follow confusing detour signs. Leila was now used to parking near a dumpster behind her bungalow. It no longer bothered her.

When she walked through the door, Brie looked up from a textbook she was lining in yellow highlighter. "Tough day?"

Seeing the girl crushed Leila's spirits. There was very little work for her to do. She spent the bulk of her time prepping for class, which Leila encouraged. Increasingly, she believed the only reason she was keeping Brie on the payroll was to avoid feeling completely isolated and alone.

Leila slumped onto a red leather armchair. She'd put so much care in picking stylish office furniture, imagining an endless stream of clients. What an idiot she'd been. Her disappointment was a noose around her neck. She was losing hope that Miller would ever settle on a house. With no other deals in the works, she'd have to charge another month's expenses on a card.

"Did you get my text?" Brie asked.

"Nope. What's up? Is it free margarita night at the bar?"

"You've been invited to the opening of Ten Twenty Biscayne."

Leila sat up. Ten Twenty was Raul Reyes's new building. For months, construction cranes had crowded lower Biscayne as a modern high-rise materialized opposite the bay. It was the first sign that Reyes, having completely transformed the Design District from a run-down neighborhood to an all-around, high-end luxury destination, had turned his attention to the downtown area.

"They just called. It's tonight at six."

It was half past three. "Talk about short notice!"

"I said you'd be there. Free margaritas can wait."

She thanked Brie and sent her home. She had to shower, choose an outfit, straighten her hair and head downtown ahead of rush hour traffic. Before she did anything, though, she called Sofia.

As she excitedly shared the news, she was suddenly cut down at the knees. "I can't go!"

"Wait… What?" Sofia said, confused.

"Nick is behind this."

Two weeks had passed without any word from him, and she'd assumed he'd gone back to New York. But this last minute invite had his fingerprints all over it.

"Why is that a problem?" Sofia asked. "You handled it last time."

"I didn't handle it well."

"How did you leave things?"

"Messy." *Real* messy.

"Get it together," Sofia ordered. "This is no time for a meltdown. If we hid from every man we had a little history with, where would that leave us?"

Unfortunately, Leila was in full meltdown mode, on the edge of her bed with her head between her knees. This was how it was going to be from here on out. Nick was back and avoiding him would require acrobatic skills. As the realization settled like rocks in the pit of her stomach, she closed her eyes and tuned out Sofia, who was poking fun.

Somehow Leila had tricked herself into thinking their last encounter was a dream, haunting but ultimately inconsequential. The circumstances were certainly dreamy—an extravagant party at a romantic site, an enchanted garden, a hidden cave—these were not the elements of real life. And how often had she dreamed about Nick, only to wake up alone and have to get on with life? But Sofia was right. She had to handle it, find a way to deal with him. Denial was not a strategy.

Nick's strategy was simple: lure Leila out of hiding.

Everything had fallen into place for him and he was starting to believe the myth of his own luck. Reyes had made the offer. He'd accepted on the spot, joining his team as an associate of Kane & Madison. Connie, thrilled with such a high profile partnership, agreed to his immediate transfer.

The one thing that hadn't fallen into place was Leila. He was surprised to learn she hadn't been invited to the open house, but a phone call had fixed that. He knew she'd come. Nothing would keep her from it. Nothing would keep him from her. He had a hundred questions and tonight, he wanted answers.

Chapter 20

When Leila arrived downtown, the late January sun was still warm. A perky hostess greeted her in the building's luxurious ground-floor lobby, handing her a glossy brochure. "There's champagne on the Sky Terrace. The model unit is on the twenty-fifth floor. But also feel free to explore our gym, pool and spa."

Leila rode up to the Sky Terrace and wasted half an hour searching for Nick. When she was satisfied he wasn't hiding among the guests or behind the potted palm trees, she took a breath and dove into the elegant cocktail party. Her objective was to meet the right people, distribute her cards like propaganda leaflets and maybe even score an audience with the king himself who, like Nick, was noticeably absent.

Then she bumped into Paige. This time Paige took the time to introduce her to a few people, real heavy hitters. Interacting with them proved difficult. Conversations swirled around their latest sales and the trophy listings they'd scored. Leila gladly offered the one thing they were all privately seeking. Praise.

"That's impressive!... Wow!... I'm familiar with that property and it's amazing."

After a couple of glasses of champagne, she mellowed out and started having fun. It wasn't until someone asked what she thought of the model unit that it occurred to her she'd missed the point of the party. She was here to check out the goods.

Sandra Villanueva, a well-known industry veteran, gave Leila a guided tour of the model unit. It wasn't the grand spread depicted in the brochure. The space was tight and the layout awkward. Leila didn't know anyone who'd pay half a million dollars for it. But Sandra knew how to play up the positive. She gushed over the sleek design of the kitchen with its lipstick-red cabinets, stainless-steel this and that, and honed-granite countertop. *Honed granite!* Because polished granite was too common, too expected and just not special enough for Ten Twenty Biscayne.

They stepped out onto the balcony that overlooked six rows of traffic on Biscayne Boulevard and the park that curved along the bay. The air was fine and the altitude buffered the city sounds. Sandra pointed to the horizon and said that when the sun rose over the water it was like nothing Leila could ever imagine. She tried to imagine it, anyway, and saw herself at eye level with the rising sun—a flat, copper disc pinned to a lavender sky. She imagined grabbing it and pocketing it like a penny.

"How would you like to wake up to this view every morning?" Sandra asked.

Leila leaned on the balcony rail and sighed with longing. Considering she'd woken up in a somber room to the sound of a drill cutting through asphalt, she'd absolutely love it.

"I'll take over from here."

With that she was pulled back to reality. Nick was standing inside the glass door in his signature midnight-blue suit. Seeing him in the light of day was a shock, drawing him out of the dream realm once and for all.

"Great!" Sandra exclaimed. "I'm heading down before there's nothing left to eat."

Leila glanced at Sandra, silently pleading with her not to leave, but the woman tapped her arm. "I'm leaving you in good hands. Nicolas Adrian is our sales director and he's phenomenal."

Nick waited for Sandra to collect her things before shutting the balcony door. They were alone and the fastest way out was a quick drop twenty-five flights down.

"I was beginning to think you weren't coming," he said.

"I was beginning to think you weren't here."

"You're not getting off that easily," Nick said. "I thought we could talk now, since last time we got distracted."

"There's really nothing to talk about."

"You owe me an explanation."

"I don't *owe* you anything."

The glass door slid open and a familiar face poked through. It was Raquel. Good old Raquel of South of Fifth.

"You crazy kids… Talk about déjà vu all over again." Her plump lips were twisted in a smirk.

Leila watched as Nick lost his solemn expression and turned on the charm. A slow smile brought light to his marble-blue eyes. "Hello, stranger."

"When did you get back?" Raquel asked.

"Not long," Nick said.

Whatever that meant, Leila noted that he hadn't bothered to contact her. If they hadn't run into each other at Reyes's party, they might not have met at all. And now he was all *You owe me an explanation*. Really?

"It's late, I should go," Leila said. "Good seeing you, Raquel."

Without a glance toward Nick, she breezed past the other woman. The last thing she heard before slamming the front door shut behind her was Raquel's abrasive voice. "How about you show me around?"

Leila rode the elevator straight down to the lobby and, after languishing in line at the valet booth, changed her mind and darted across all six lanes of traffic toward the park. Although the sun had set, the park was alive with children playing tag and yoga enthusiasts in spandex toting rolled-up mats. She found an empty bench near the central fountain, which happened to be dead and dry.

How am I supposed to deal with this?

She was a mess, torn between wanting to kiss him and

to kick him in the groin. When she spotted him approaching in the distance, she came close to tears. Was there no escaping him?

Nick joined her on the bench. The fountain suddenly came alive, sending a column of water into the night.

"I'm getting tired of chasing you," he said.

"Then stop."

"Give me answers and I might."

Leila turned to him. "Okay. Let's get this over with. What do you want to know?"

"Why did you run away?"

"Just now?"

"Leila…" Her name was a one-word warning. "Why couldn't I reach you after I left for New York? Where did you go? Why did you run?"

"I didn't run away. I went to stay with my aunt in Naples for a few months."

"How was I supposed to know that? You disconnected your phone."

"I changed carriers."

"You never once called me."

"I was busy getting my broker's license, starting my business."

"Stop messing with me."

"What do you want me to tell you?"

"Tell me you got hit on the head after I left. Nothing you're saying makes sense."

"You got promoted and I got fired! Does that make sense?" she yelled, drawing looks from trendy moms pushing state-of-the-art strollers.

"What?"

He looked and sounded genuinely bewildered.

"It's real simple. I got fired. Didn't Jo-Ann tell you?"

"No," Nick said. "But why should I have had to ask Jo-Ann anything? Jo-Ann wasn't my lover."

His outburst betrayed his anger and his pain. Leila braced her heart against guilt. She'd earned the right to be selfish. "Sorry if I was less than gracious about it. But I had to take care of myself."

"She *fired* you? After she'd said she wouldn't."

"And she wasted no time. Your plane hadn't even landed at JFK."

"Leila, we could've fought this."

"Oh, Nick! Please." There was nothing to fight. She was let go when her services were no longer needed. But the look on Jo-Ann's face had told a very different story. "She knew about us. And, I don't blame you, but God knows discretion wasn't your thing."

"Sounds like blame to me," Nick said flatly. "Did you stop to think you could've joined me? Like I wanted you to?"

"Because I had nothing better to do, right? I was out of a job, so why not follow a man I barely knew to a whole other state?"

"You barely knew me?"

They sat in silence. Nick stood to leave.

She instinctively reached for his arm to stop him. He was right. It was time they had it out. No more running and hiding. "Don't go. We're talking like you wanted. It's not my fault you don't like what I have to say."

"None of this is what I wanted."

"Nick—"

"I'm sorry, Leila, for what you went through. But you broke me. I hope it was worth it."

He walked away, leaving her among the kids playing tag, the yogis and the trendy moms. These light and frothy people made her feel dark and heavy.

A teenage girl whizzed past on a skateboard and hollered, "*Girrrl*, he told you!"

Chapter 21

There were days when the forces at play in Leila's life were more constricting than a pair of Spanx. Her morning started with a call from Cedar Oaks, her aunt's nursing home. She sat up in bed, her heart pounding. The prior year's hardships weren't limited to her love and work life. Her family life had collapsed, as well, with the sudden downturn of her aunt's health. But since Hurricane Nick had hit her shores, she'd forgotten to check up on Camille.

"Is everything okay?" Leila asked, cutting through the usual endless formalities.

Everything was fine, the nurse assured her, except that her aunt had had a near-syncope episode.

"A near what?"

Now and again, she questioned her choice of Cedar Oaks, a pricey facility way out in the suburb of Weston. It had a stellar reputation, and she'd picked it over more affordable and accessible state-run homes. The property was beautiful and clean. The halls forever smelled of freshly cut flowers. But, man, did they love to blow up her phone, calling to inform her about one mishap after another. It was good to be informed, but why couldn't they *prevent* the mishaps from happening in the first place? At the rate they were depleting her aunt's savings and pension, it was the least they could do.

"She fainted," the nurse said. "Well, nearly. Her doctor visited and adjusted her blood pressure medication."

"She'll be all right?"

"She'll be fine," the nurse said. "But there's one more thing."

There was always one more thing.

"She injured her arm. When she *nearly* loss consciousness, she rolled off her wheelchair and fell onto her left arm."

Leila held her phone away from her ear and let out a silent cry. She wondered what had happened to the woman who could strut across a room in four-inch heels. That woman didn't fall out of wheelchairs or have near-anything episodes.

"Miss Amis, are you still there?"

Leila apologized and asked whether her aunt had sprained anything or broken any bones.

"No, it's just a bruise. We assure you…"

She stopped listening. She preferred to gather nursing home intelligence through the army of nurse assistants.

"I'll stop by and see for myself."

She was all set to meet with Miller at noon; afterward, she was free. She checked the time. *Holy crap!* It was half past ten. After a sleepless night, it appeared she'd fallen into a coma. Just then, she heard footsteps in the front room and caught the aroma of coffee drifting into her bedroom. Brie had already clocked in.

Brie was in the kitchen, rinsing out her coffee mug. Leila didn't like her assistant seeing her this way, barefoot, in a T-shirt, and her hair in a messy ponytail. Usually she was dressed and ready for work by the time the girl showed up. She yearned for privacy, but she desperately needed coffee.

"Wow," Brie said, eyeing her with a smile. "That party must've been all kinds of fun."

"Good morning, and it wasn't as much fun as you think."

"You're going to have to get it together and quick. Miller emailed to confirm your twelve o'clock. He said to meet him at his office."

Showing Miller yet another property for him to bulldoze

wasn't a pleasant way to start an already crummy day, but what else did she have to do?

"Is there anything else on the calendar?" she asked hopefully. Maybe she'd missed something.

Brie shook her head no. "Which brings me to what I've wanted to talk to you about. Maybe you should consider *not* paying me this week. Or next."

Leila looked at the girl as if she'd grown a second head. Had she heard her right? "That's not how it works, Brie. Employees ask for raises and bonuses. Not the opposite."

"You can't afford it," Brie said matter-of-factly.

"Of course I can!" Leila cried.

"We both know you can't."

Leila launched into a feminist tirade to better hide her humiliation, ending with "You should always be compensated for your work."

"We both know I don't really work here. I do homework."

"That's not the point."

"The only reason I'm working here is to keep my folks happy. They're old school and still think a job builds character."

"They're right!"

"They're wrong. I don't *need* a job. I've been earning money off my blog since high school."

"A blog is not a job."

"It's better than a job. My car is better than yours."

Leila snapped. "Oh, please! You drive a Ford Fiesta."

"It's brand new with power everything plus Navigation and Bluetooth. Does your car even know what Bluetooth is?"

"Has anyone told you you're a brat?"

"All the time," Brie said. "But seriously, don't worry about me. I can skip a payday or two."

The doorbell rang and both women, unaccustomed to visitors, jumped.

Brie rested her coffee cup on the counter. "I ordered toner. Probably UPS."

Leila, eager to table the discussion, shuffled off to the bathroom. "I'm going to shower. Don't want to be late for my one appointment of the day."

While brushing her teeth, she checked her attitude. This meeting with Miller was a needed distraction. Instead of dreading it, she'd embrace it. He was annoying enough to force her out of her head. She couldn't obsess over Nick while dealing with him. This was crucial because last night her emotional landscape had changed its colors. She was no longer sure of her position. Had she done the smart thing or made the mistake of her life? Had she hurt Nick? Did she owe him an apology, if nothing else?

Absent a moral high ground, she was at a disadvantage.

She showered, wrapped a towel around her chest and returned to the kitchen for the coffee she hadn't had a chance to pour. After rummaging through the fridge for creamer and coming up empty, she called out to Brie. "Are we out of creamer? And don't say I can't afford it!"

She reached for a container of Greek yogurt well past its expiration date and tossed it in the trash. She needed to get to the supermarket.

Brie cried out to her, "Don't know! And don't come out here!"

"Why not?" Did the UPS guy stay to install the toner?

A third voice rose up, calm and sure. "Because she doesn't want me to see you naked."

While Brie erupted in giggles, Leila broke out in goose bumps. She slammed the refrigerator door and, clutching the knot of her towel to her chest, raced down the hall to the front room. Nick was seated comfortably opposite

Brie, Starbucks coffee cup in hand. Funny, he didn't look broken to her.

"Nick, what are you doing here?"

This was a true surprise considering the way he'd stormed off last night. She hadn't expected him to reach out to her again, or so soon.

"He brought you coffee," Brie answered sweetly on his behalf. "A latte. You won't need creamer."

"Trust me, he can speak for himself."

Was he trying to make her nostalgic for mornings when he'd brought her coffee at her desk? Leila took a breath. Why was she even thinking about that?

"I need to speak to you," he said.

She needed to speak with him, too. But not now and not like this. "I don't have time. I'm getting ready to meet a client."

"I see that."

The look in his eyes caused her temperature to spike. Her fingers tightened around the knot of her towel. Maybe she should've gone through the trouble of putting on a robe before rushing out.

Nick rose and handed her the lidded cup, their fingers brushing. She was upset, but not enough to turn down good coffee.

"Get dressed," he said. "I'll wait."

"And I'll keep him company," Brie chimed.

Feeling outnumbered in her own home/office, Leila locked herself in her bedroom. *Hold it together.*

She flung open her closet, skipping over outfits she'd normally wear on an ordinary weekday, searching for something punchier. It took some effort, but she retrieved her red DVF wrap dress. It was a few years old but still a classic. It had always helped her feel confident. She slipped it on, pretending to have forgotten all about Nick's expressed wish to unwrap the wrap.

When she returned to the front room feeling in control, feeling like a boss, she found Brie was in confession mode. The young girl was sharing with Nick her concerns for her future.

"If you're looking for a job," Nick said, "give me a call. I can help."

Leila lost it. The man was like a weed invading her garden. "Hello! She *has* a job. A job she apparently doesn't even need."

"He meant after graduation," Brie said hastily. "That's a long time off."

"I told you, Brie. He can speak for himself."

Leila felt less like a boss and more like a grump. She couldn't handle Nick, couldn't function normally around him.

Brie mumbled an apology and traded knowing glances with Nick. How was it possible they'd forged an alliance in so little time?

Leila asked Nick into her office, mostly to get him away from her assistant. She couldn't let him snag the one person on her team.

Once the door was closed behind them she said, "Nick, listen, I don't mean to be rude—"

"So don't."

"I have to be in the Gables by noon."

"I drove through construction traffic and left my new car out in an alley to see you today."

"You could've called."

"I wanted to speak to you in person."

Leila riffled through a pile of printouts on her desk for the day's listing. Nick picked up a picture frame and asked, "Is this your aunt? The one you told me about?"

She snatched the frame out of his hands. "We don't have time for small talk. My client is a jerk. If I show up late or give him any other excuse to drop me, he will."

"Drop you?"

She realized, with a pinch of envy, that the concept was foreign to him. "He's made all kinds of threats."

Nick's demeanor, even his posture, changed. "What's his problem?"

He was the brightest in the business. She'd be a fool to not pick his brain.

"He wants the impossible. He's holding out for an updated four-bedroom in Coral Gables proper and won't shell out more than five hundred grand. Yesterday, I showed him a fixer with a ton of potential and he hated it. The one I'm showing him today is no better, but I'm running out of options."

"Who is he? What does he do?"

"He's a tax attorney, relocating from Atlanta."

How many times had Miller waxed poetic about the fabulous mini-mansions his money could buy in Atlanta? He'd described palatial homes on oversize lots with random extras like mudrooms, rec rooms and bonus rooms.

Nick ran his fingers through his hair. "He's got unrealistic expectations."

"Exactly!"

"He needs a reality check."

"How do I do that?"

"Show him the house you know he wants, but can't afford."

"I can't play games. He'll just get pissed."

Nick faced her, his expression stern. "Leila, you run this deal. Not the other way around."

They were slipping into their old roles. Even after all this time, and the effort she'd put into starting her own business, she was still the protégée and he the mentor.

"Okay. I show him his dream house, tell him what it costs, he blows up and then what?"

"He calms the hell down."

"And if he doesn't?"

"You tell him the truth—he's wasting *your* time."

"But I need—" She stopped herself from oversharing. Having forgotten how easy it was to confide in him, she was in no position to judge Brie.

"I know," he said. "But you can't let him walk all over you."

It was too late to stop that; Miller's footprints were all over her back. But she trusted Nick's instincts. Since her methods had led nowhere, it was worth a shot.

"Okay." She powered up her computer. "Help me find something outrageous."

They worked quickly together. Within minutes, they'd found the perfect property and contacted the listing agent. Nick offered to accompany her and she happily accepted. It was only right that he be there to help clean up the mess when it all hit the fan.

Out in the alley, both she and Nick reached for their keys. Next to her Mazda and Brie's Ford was a gunmetal-gray Maserati, as muscular as a car can get.

Nick said, "Let's take my car."

"From Mercedes to Maserati? That's a jump."

He held open the passenger door, revealing indulgent chocolate-brown leather seats. "I did okay in New York."

"I'm sure you did."

Leila slid on her sunglasses to hide the twinkle in her eyes. The sexy interior was making her very, very happy. The bonus was watching Nick drive it. She loved how he handled Miami's chaotic roads; focused, one hand on the wheel. Once again she felt the dangerous pull of nostalgia taking her back to a time when watching Nick was all she'd wanted to do. She cleared her throat and tried to move the conversation forward.

"Aren't I taking you away from your own work? What do you do for Reyes, anyway?"

The second question was the important one. If he'd done so well in New York, why leave? How could Miami compete?

"I'm here to sell out the Ten Twenty building, and fast. Otherwise, Reyes's reputation takes a hit. And he knows it."

"We all have our problems, I guess." It sounded like big business. "Still chasing the money, huh?"

"You used to like that about me," he said.

"Did I?"

"I talked to Paige. She says you're looking for work."

Leila did her best to look cool. "I gave her my card. No big deal."

"Do you need work?"

"I'm fine. Thanks."

She looked out the window. They'd veered onto the Julia Tuttle Causeway and, as always, the multimillion-dollar homes on Star Island made her heart soar.

"I'll put in a good word for you with the old man, maybe for some future project."

"Is that what you call him? The old man?"

Nick grinned. "He loves me like a son."

"Does everyone love you?"

"You tell me."

They carried on like this, teasing and taunting. Before she knew it, they were cruising down US-1 and nearing Miller's law firm on Ponce de Leon. She called to let him know she was five minutes away. Still, she expected him to keep them waiting for about fifteen minutes more.

Nick parked curbside and Leila unfastened her seat belt. "I'll give him the front seat. His ego won't fit in the back."

"I'll get in the back," Nick said. "You drive."

"What?" The offer left her flustered and more than a little excited. "You're trusting me with your new toy?"

He stepped out of the car, giving up the prized driver's

seat. "You need to look like you're in charge. That won't happen if you're stuck in the back."

She wasted no time getting behind the wheel. He helped her adjust the seat then settled in the back. Grabbing hold of the leather-wrapped transmission gear, she said, "This feels good!"

"You look good."

Leila pushed her sunglasses to the top of her head and she and Nick locked eyes in the rearview mirror. Even relegated to the back seat, there was no mistaking that he was in charge.

"I need you to be on your best behavior," she said.

"You'll hardly know I'm here."

Impossible, she thought. He looked beyond handsome in a light blue shirt, dark gray pants and the leather belt she'd so adeptly unfastened that night in the cave.

"I'm sorry I walked away last night," he said.

This was the talk, then. The lunch hour crowd started to pour onto the sidewalks. The car with its tinted windows offered a private, quiet space.

"It wasn't completely unjustified," she said.

"I still can't figure why you froze me out."

"Nick, if I hurt you—"

"Let's clear that up. There's no *if*."

Startled by the force of his reaction, Leila went quiet.

"Last night you said you barely knew me." He drilled on. "What the hell is that?"

"Nick, I'm—"

"You're sorry?"

The word sounded hollow. "You don't know what I was going through."

"I came looking for you, Leila. I came back precisely because I wanted to know what you were going through."

"Nick, I *am* sorry."

Her voice cracked and, to her horror, her eyes began to

well with tears. Having spent months hating him, now she hated herself. He lunged forward and reached for a pack of tissues in the glove compartment.

"Dry your eyes," he said. "Your client will think I'm being mean to you."

"Aren't you?" She pulled a compact from her purse and carefully dabbed at her smudged mascara.

"Look, maybe we both messed up. I know I gave up on you way too soon." He proposed a neat solution. "Forgive and forget?"

Leila looked up and found that his gaze had never left her face. What was he thinking? Did he expect them to skip over the past like a shallow puddle? How realistic was that?

Just then Miller charged out of the office building, looking frumpy in his boxy business suit. For the first time, Leila wasn't afraid of him.

Pointing out the window, she said, "There's my client."

Nick's thick brows drew close as he sized Miller up. "You've been running around with this guy for how long now?"

"Correction. I've been *catering* to my client's needs for about five months. His contract is almost up."

Leila stepped out to greet Miller. He eyed the car. "Had to call for backup?"

"Not at all. But if you don't mind, my friend Nicolas Adrian will be joining us today."

With both men in the car, Miller in the passenger seat and Nick a shadowy presence in the back, Leila worried she'd choke on an excess of testosterone.

Miller fastened his seat belt, frowning even as he nodded his approval. "This is a far cry from your little Mazda, huh?"

"Hey," Leila said, "I love my car."

"As you should," Nick said.

Miller glanced at him for the first time. "You two know each other long?"

"I barely know her," Nick said.

"Don't listen to him," Leila said with a short laugh. "We go way back. I used to work—"

Nick cut her off. "We worked at the same agency. We were a team."

Miller waited for her to corroborate Nick's version of the facts.

Leila nodded slowly. Sometimes she missed working with him more than anything.

The two-story Colonial occupied a double lot surrounded by a precisely trimmed hedge. A glossy red front door opened to a light-filled space with beige walls and a tawny pine floor. The listing agent allowed them access and pointed out the updated kitchen with traditional touches: a swan-neck faucet dipping into a copper sink and an oversize hood hovering over the gas stove. The second floor offered a spacious master bedroom, en suite bath and endless closets, which was unheard of in similar homes. The current owners were a pair of savvy developers who'd pulled off the impossible: increasing the square footage by tacking on an addition, all without destroying the home's authentic charm.

"The last house on this street sold for one million flat," she told Miller. "This one is listed at one point three. The price reflects the double lot and master suite. It's even got a three-car garage. Detached, but still. What do you think?"

"I don't know," Miller said. "It's a great house."

Leila was shocked that the price alone hadn't fired him up. Was he showing off for Nick?

"Give me a minute to call my wife, will you?"

"We'll be out in the yard."

The listing agent stayed behind in the kitchen. Nick followed Leila down a brick path toward a hidden orchard.

"Calling the wife is a good sign," she said.

"Or he's looking for an out," Nick said. "What do you think about the house?"

"I think it's lovely. How about you?"

"Not my style."

"Let me guess. It's missing a sea wall, a dock and a boat lift."

In the calm of the orchard he said, "See how well you know me?"

Sunlight streamed in from all sides of the orchard, highlighting the rust tones of Nick's hair. Her first impression still held: the man was trouble.

Miller saved her. "Hey!" he called out. "Where are you two?"

Nick's jaw tightened. "Do me a favor. Find that man a house and get rid of him."

She gestured for him to shut up, and darted off. For the moment, Miller was her only actual client.

She found him waiting by the pool. He'd stripped off his heavy suit jacket, revealing a white shirt stained with sweat.

"So what do you think?" Leila asked Miller.

"I talked to my wife, even sent her some photos. It's a solid house."

"Positive feedback! From you, that's big."

"Not so fast. Love the look, don't love the price."

"The two go hand in hand."

"I'd go for it, but my wife isn't sold. She says it's too much house."

Blaming the wife… Nick had called it. "Did you show her the closet? And the kitchen? It's everything she asked for."

"She sort of liked the old house we saw yesterday."

What's happening? "You can't mean 'Grandma's house'?"

"She says she can make that old place look just as good as this one."

Leila nearly fainted. "Of course she can. What did I tell you?"

This sudden turnaround validated her efforts. Grandma's house was the right fit, and *she*'d called it. Leila looked around for Nick. He'd stayed behind, giving her space, but she'd have liked to share this miracle with him.

"You women think alike. What can I say?"

"I'd have to call the agent to see if it's even available. It was priced right."

"You've got work to do," Miller said. "Get your boyfriend back here."

Chapter 22

They dropped off her client and Nick had Leila to himself again. She was flush with excitement, and so pretty he wanted to kiss her at every traffic stop. But she wanted to talk business. Miller was prepared to pay the full asking price. However, Nick suggested she start low and shave off fifty grand. Miller was cheap, and if she could save him even a dime, he'd be loyal to her forever. She called the listing agent just as they pulled up to her office. With a steady voice, she said, "My client is prepared to offer four hundred and fifty thousand contingent on inspection." If Nick remembered correctly, Miller's exact words were, "I want to inspect the shit out of that house."

Brie had left for the day and it was just the two of them when the agent called with a counter offer. Leila sat at her desk, looking nervous.

Nick took a seat and encouraged her with a nod.

She answered the call on speaker. "What do you have for me?"

"We counter at four seventy-five."

Leila looked directly at him. He recognized that look in her eyes, a glow of satisfaction that followed a big win.

"I think that can work," she said. "We have a deal. I'll get the paperwork to you."

She hung up. "We did it!"

Nick felt a rush. When he got the job with Reyes he hadn't been this excited. He hadn't been excited at all. Taking the job had been a power move to get him where he wanted to be. This relatively smaller deal felt like a personal victory and reminded him why he loved working with Leila. "You did it, babe."

"This is my first major deal," she said, breathless. "I know it's small potatoes to you—"

"It's not." He leaned forward in his chair. "How does it feel to win?"

Leila held his gaze. Then she circled the desk, leaned over to kiss him.

He stopped her, pulling away slightly. "You're on a high. You're not thinking."

She touched a fingertip to his lips. "You asked how it feels. This is how it feels. Like old times."

Nostalgia won the day. Nothing was resolved between them; Nick knew it. She'd said she was sorry but what about? But what did he care when she was leaning over him, running her fingers through his hair.

He reached for and unfastened the tie of her dress. "You've finally worn it for me."

She tilted her head back. "You remember everything."

"Everything."

He kissed her neck, revisiting known trigger spots. She whispered in his ear, "So do I."

With a groan of impatience, he lifted her off his lap and onto her desk. He brushed aside the front panels of her dress and stopped a beat to take in his handiwork. The black-mesh bra and matching panties were worthy of the grand reveal. He saw the chocolate disc of a nipple and went savage, lowering his mouth to suck it through the sheer fabric.

Leila tried to slow him down. "Wait. Let's go to my room."

"No." He rested a palm on the clear space just beneath her throat and pressed until her back was against the desktop. "Let's go right here."

"Whatever you want."

"Is that right?"

He reached between her thighs, thumbed aside the delicate underwear but held back from touching her. She twisted and let out a plaintive moan. A pencil holder went toppling onto the floor.

"Leila…?"

"Yes."

"What do you want?"

She raised her hips slightly. "Touch me."

He obliged her, wanting nothing more than to feel her come alive under his touch again.

All Nick wanted was to exhaust her. They moved from her office to the kitchen for a quick break to share a glass of water. Then he bent her over the sink, drove into her and paused, giving into the headiest feeling in the world. Leila moaned and he picked up the pace. Her cries of "Yes! God, yes!" were muffled by all the construction noise. When they collapsed, sweaty and out of breath, she kept at it, gasping, "Oh, God! Oh, God! Oh, God!"

"Shh…" He kissed the delicate skin just behind her ears. "Don't want to be indiscrete."

The sharp look she gave him was proof that she'd felt the jab. Then she crawled away from him and he regretted the stupid remark.

"Thirsty?" she asked.

"Do you have anything stronger than water?"

She opened her freezer and pulled out a bottle of Grey Goose.

"You're so grown up now."

"Someone taught me the value of a well-stocked bar."

She splashed some vodka into a tumbler and handed it to him. Nick approached, dragged the cold glass along her bare arm and watched her shiver. "There must have been others."

"Other what?"

"Other men who taught you things."

"That sounds very chauvinistic."

"Why not just answer the question?"

She leaned against her kitchen table. "I haven't asked what you were up to in New York."

"Ask and I'll tell you."

She shrugged. "I don't want to know."

Her evasiveness worried him and he drew his own conclusions. "I hope you had fun."

"To fun!" She raised her glass in a toast, thanked him for a good time then she asked him to leave.

"You want me to go?" he repeated as if he hadn't understood.

"I have to be somewhere. Fun time is over."

"When will I see you again?"

"I don't know. Call me."

"Call you tonight?"

"No. Not tonight."

"Got it."

The glassy look in her eyes told him it was all an act, but still it stung. Nick dressed. His anger made him agile and he was out the door before she could say another word. This was a new low for him. No matter what anyone thought about him, he'd never asked a woman to leave his apartment while she was still hot from sex. As he backed out of the alley behind Leila's house, he vowed he never would.

Chapter 23

With last week's roses in the trash and this week's irises arranged in a glass vase, Leila sat at her aunt's bedside. Camille stared at her with lucid eyes, but it was an illusion. Her mind was far gone, her thoughts looped around a single spindle. Time and place were mysteries to her, but she remembered most people. She remembered Leila, at least. Lung cancer, both the disease and the treatment, had wrecked her. Her skin fell away from her frame in thin, brown sheets as fine as Phyllo dough. Her once-thick black hair had the texture of cotton candy, dissolvable to the touch. The rest of her body vanished under the thin sheet.

Lately, Leila's days were structured around the hour or two she could spare to visit with her aunt.

The visits always began with Camille pointing to a Bible on the bedside table. It served no other purpose but to hold a collection of photographs. Tucked within Genesis were two black-and-white photographs and several Polaroid prints of her aunt at various stages of her life. Two-year-old Camille in diapers, a big red bow in her hair. At fifteen in a blue chiffon dress. At nineteen in her first wedding gown. At twenty-nine in more modern bridal attire: a mini-dress with fluted sleeves.

Camille had no children, a fact that had somehow factored into the end of her marriages. But she never dwelled on that. Instead she began her stories with, "My dear... I used to be a knockout."

"I know it," Leila would reply. It was the only charitable thing to do.

This time, the story was over before it began. Camille was seized by a fit of coughs that left her breathless and exhausted. Leila fit the oxygen tube into her flared nostrils. Within minutes, her aunt fell asleep; her jaw slacked open to reveal a pale tongue and missing teeth.

Leila slipped the photos one by one into the yellowed pages of the Bible and tiptoed out the door. In the hall she ran into Dr. Passakos, the medical director.

"Ms. Amis," he said. "Good to see you. If you don't mind, I'd like a word."

Dr. Passakos was an ancient ruin. He could check into the nursing home as a resident at any time.

"I signed everything," Leila said hastily. There was no end to the number of forms she'd had to sign and date.

"Everything is in order," he said. "That's not what I want to talk to you about. I'd like to discuss the notion of hospice care."

"Hospice?" Was he talking about putting Camille down like a horse?

Dr. Passakos reached out to touch her shoulder, but then appeared to change his mind. "Your aunt is ready and eligible for end-of-life services. My recommendation is that you approve transfer of care. It's for the best. But we shouldn't discuss this out in the open. Do you have a minute?"

Her phone rang, giving her a much needed out. "Not today. Super busy."

"When?" Dr. Passakos asked patiently, revealing his experience in dealing with difficult, even irrational, people.

"Soon," she said. "I promise."

Leila escaped the building, finding relief in the morning heat. The phone had stopped ringing but started right back up again. It was Sofia.

"Are you getting ready?" Sofia asked.

"For what?"

"The luncheon for the homeless."

Leila groaned. She'd agreed to it last week, bought the ticket and forgotten all about it.

"If you leave me hanging," Sofia said. "I swear…"

"Calm down!" If the choice were between rallying to end homelessness and discussing hospice with Dr. Passakos, she'd happily pick the former over the latter. "I'll be there. Where is it again?"

"JW Marriott. One o'clock."

With no time to waste, she drove straight downtown and applied lipstick in traffic. In her silk polka-dot blouse and dark skinny jeans, she wasn't necessarily dressed for a charity luncheon, but she had a spare pair of heels in the trunk of her car. To avoid the cost of valet, she parked at a meter and walked the rest of the way.

Sofia was waiting in the grand lobby looking stylish in a beige sheath dress and leopard-print pumps. These events were her hunting grounds, where she met the women wealthy enough to afford her services.

"Here I am!" Leila called out.

Sofia looked up from her phone, took in Leila's outfit and said, "You really were going to stand me up. I can't believe you!"

"Sorry, but life got crazy. I totally forgot."

"Fine. You can tell me all about it over a three-course lunch."

They rode the elevator to the ballroom. It was the usual setup: a sign-in table with an assortment of brochures and complimentary pens. A volunteer offered to help find their name tags. She approached Leila. "And your last name is?"

"Amis. Leila Amis."

"Why does that sound familiar?"

Leila studied the redhead behind the table and dropped the complimentary pen she'd swept up. The name tag pinned to the woman's chest read Monica Rivers. "You're Nick's Monica!"

The redhead laughed wholeheartedly and Leila could

have died with embarrassment. The words had popped out before her mind had had a chance to edit them.

"It's been a long time since anyone has called me that! But, yes, I was Nicolas Adrian's assistant for years. And you're the one who replaced me. I've been dying to meet you."

Sofia and Monica knew each other from the days Monica worked with Nick, and they greeted each other warmly.

"It's a small world!" Sofia exclaimed. "You've met Leila."

Monica nodded. "We have so much in common, we ought to sit and talk."

"You really should," Sofia said.

"Maybe after lunch," Leila said. *Or maybe never...*

"Or maybe right now," Sofia suggested.

"Why not?" Monica said.

"Oh, but you're busy," Leila said.

"Forget that! I've been on my feet all morning. Plus the keynote speaker is running late. We've got time."

Monica announced to her colleagues that she was taking a short break. Then the three women found a quiet place to talk at a nearby lounge area. Sofia sat between them and, like a talk show host, set the tone.

"Have you heard, Red? Nick is back."

Leila cut Sofia a sideways glance. *Red?* So what? They had pet names for each other.

"Really? Is he still with K&M?" she asked. "I wonder who's on his team."

"Not me," Leila said.

Monica's smile was polite, hinting that she knew the whole dirty story.

Leila flushed.

Monica reached out and touched her arm. "I've heard so much about you. All my friends at the office said you were beautiful. And they were so jealous. You got the plum assignment. Everyone wanted to work with Nick."

"The big mystery is why you ever left," Leila said.

"That's no mystery. The job was great before I had my twins." Monica handed over her phone. The screen displayed a picture of kindergarten-age boys. They weren't the copper-haired darlings Leila had imagined, but sandy-blond daredevils hanging upside down from monkey bars. "I couldn't keep up with the long hours. Nick was fine with it. He let me go home early nearly every day. Then Jo-Ann found out and we had it out. Long story short—"

"She fired you."

"Right, you've been there," Monica said. "She shows up at your desk with a box… Dreadful."

They'd both gone through the same experience but for very different reasons. Where Leila had wanted more time alone with Nick, Monica had only wanted more time with her children.

"Nick pissed her off," Monica said, "and you had to pay the price. That was tough luck."

"How do you mean?" Sofia asked.

"By pulling rank and demanding she keep you on at the agency," Monica explained. "Who knows? If he hadn't interfered you might've still had a job there."

Leila fell back in her seat. If Monica's version of the facts was true, it changed things. It meant she hadn't lost her job because of her relationship with Nick. Well, it *did*, but it didn't—not the way she'd thought.

"How is Nick, by the way?" Monica asked.

"Better than ever," Leila replied.

"Tell him to call me," Monica said.

Leila promised that she would…whenever she ever got around to returning Nick's calls. She hated playing phone tag, but believed it necessary. If she weren't careful, she'd be right back where she was a year ago—dependent on him for her every pleasure, including her morning coffee. She was not going to allow him to hijack her life, not this time.

Monica stood to leave. "He found me this job, you know. And I love it, more flexible. I miss those bonuses, though."

Leila felt the need to say something kind in return for the information Monica had freely shared. "You should know he hated losing you. On my first day he was still fighting for you. For a while it was awkward."

Monica smiled proudly. "But not for too long, right?"

Sofia handed her a business card. "I do kid parties now, too."

Monica waved goodbye. "Enjoy lunch, ladies."

When she was gone, Sofia said, "It's all for the best. If they hadn't let you go, you wouldn't have branched out on your own."

Leila massaged her temples. She was going to need a stiff drink. "I hope they're serving alcohol."

"Cash bar," Sofia said. "Don't worry. I've got lots of cash."

"Good. Let's head inside."

"Slow down," Sofia said. "We're not going anywhere. There's a lot to unpack here."

Leila moaned. "I don't feel like unpacking."

"Oh, we're doing this," Sofia said. "I'm curious. How did things end?"

"At the agency? With Jo-Ann waiting for me at my desk with all my stuff boxed up. I thought that was clear."

"I mean with Nick. Why did you two split up? Was it the long distance thing?"

"It was the *firing* thing," Leila cried, exasperated.

Sofia's face lit up with understanding. "Oh! You're saying when you told him, he was like, 'Sorry. Not my problem.'"

"I never told him." *And he would've never said that.*

"How do you mean?"

"I moved back to Naples, ditched my phone, got my broker's license and turned my life around."

The tidy sentence hid a parade of horrors. That solo road trip in her tiny car cramped with all her stuff, her vision blurred with tears. At one point she'd pulled over to the side of the road to throw up, mostly water and coffee. A roadside ranger had asked if she was pregnant. When she'd finally arrived at her aunt's condo, the door was locked. She'd killed a few hours at a strip mall and ditched her phone in a dumpster behind a 7-Eleven. There'd been five text messages and six missed calls from Nick.

"Are you seriously telling me you went ghost on the man?"

"When you put it that way, it sounds harsh," Leila said. "I had to get out of there. I was overwhelmed."

"Leila! That's so cold. Not to mention rude."

"Whose side are you on?"

"I don't know anymore," Sofia said. "It sucks that you lost your job, but…"

"But nothing! That Jo-Ann person we were talking about? She made me feel like…" Leila's voice trailed off. Had Jo-Ann made her feel that way or had she felt that way all along?

"You blamed him and you made him pay."

"You don't get it. That's not…that's not what I did. Not intentionally, anyway," Leila stammered. A part of her knew that Sofia was right. She'd deliberately sought to hurt Nick. She'd wanted him to feel as terrible as she did.

"Oh, I get it," Sofia said. "I've been with the same man for the last five years. I know what payback looks like."

Chapter 24

On Sunday, Nick drove out to Key Biscayne, rented a catamaran and took it out on the bay. The wind was strong and he sailed as far out as the graffiti-stained marine stadium, a casualty of neglect and time. With some effort, and a whole lot of money, it could be restored. That wasn't true of most things.

The sun pressed down on his shoulders. He'd come out to flush his heart of disappointment. He didn't understand Leila. She claimed to love him, then took every opportunity to push him away. He'd have given up on her if it weren't so obvious she had feelings for him. Why she was intent on putting them both through this misery was the only question.

A gust of wind lifted the blue sail. Nick adjusted course and admitted to himself giving up on Leila wasn't a thing he could do. No one else knew him as well as her. She'd fallen in love with him despite his faults. His workaholic ways hadn't turned her off. His smartass attitude hadn't lessened her affection. But he'd left her, and that was the crime he was ultimately paying for.

Working to straighten the tiller, Nick shrugged off his doubts. He had to remind her of what they'd had, and convince her they could get it back. He only needed a plan.

When Nick arrived at the Reyes Realty sales office on Monday, the receptionist handed him a message from Leila. Swelling with hope, he called her straight away. She answered with a nervous chuckle. "That was fast."

"See how it works?" he said. "You call me, I call you right back.

"Sorry. I've had a busy couple of days."

"Think you can make time for me?"

"Depends. What do you have in mind?"

"I have a proposition for you."

"Nick."

She said his name with a measure of distrust, as if any proposition from him could only lead to trouble.

"I'm looking to hire a real estate agent."

"Really? Why?"

"I hate where I'm staying and it's time to buy."

"Why not do the work yourself, keep the commission?"

"I don't have time to weed out inventory. I need someone to do the legwork, and you know my tastes."

She said nothing. He swiveled around in his desk chair and took in the view of Freedom Tower rising into a hazy sky.

"Actually, Nick," she said. "Until you know for sure where you want to be long-term, renting isn't a bad idea."

"Thanks for the advice. But are you really in any position to turn down business?"

"Why do I feel there's a catch?"

"Because there is. You'll have to cater to me now."

Her laugh was throaty, sexy.

"I guess we should discuss this over dinner. Are you free tonight?"

"I can be," he said. "How about eight? At Michael's."

Michael's Genuine was the foodie destination in the Design District. One thing Nick knew, Leila loved good food.

"I don't know if we can get a reservation—"

"I can," he said. "See you there."

Nick arrived early at the restaurant. He'd considered waiting at the bar when he saw Leila crossing the street, oblivious of oncoming traffic. She looked gorgeous in a simple blush-colored dress just short enough to show off her legs. When she came to stand before him, he couldn't help himself. He grabbed her waist and kissed her full on the mouth.

She kissed back, maybe out of habit, then tried to wiggle away. He held her firmly. "I'm glad you called."

She held up a manila folder. "This is work, not a date."

"I don't know the difference."

"You're about to find out."

He guided her into the restaurant. Their table for two was cozy, guaranteeing she'd always be at arm's length. He grabbed her chair by the seat and dragged it even closer. Then he reached for her hand and she pulled away. It was going to be a fun night.

To lighten the mood he ordered champagne. The restaurant's casual vibe did not translate to casual prices. Catching her worried look, he said, "Dinner is on me."

A devious smile spread across her face. "In that case, I hear the oysters are fantastic."

"Then we'll get those, too. I'm in the mood to celebrate."

"Why?" she asked. "What's got you going?"

"Two million dollars of Reyes property in escrow as of four o'clock this afternoon."

"I hate you so much right now."

He laughed and tried for her hand again. This time she waited a few seconds before pulling away. "I didn't think I'd hear from you."

She smoothed a cloth napkin on her lap. "I have something to tell you."

Their waiter returned to fill their champagne glasses. He set the smoky-green bottle in a standing ice bucket and seemed to instinctively know to walk away.

"Do I want to hear this? Because I've given it some thought. Leila, I was wrong to grill you the other day. The past is in the past." He proposed a toast. "Here's to your secrets."

She took her glass to her lips, painted a deep coral. "You make me wish I had a few."

"So what's this about?"

"I met Monica, *your* Monica, at a charity luncheon yesterday."

"You did? How's my money-maker?" he asked, and watched Leila flinch. Still so jealous…

"She had a lot to say."

"I'm not surprised."

"She seems to think Jo-Ann let me go because you pulled rank, demanding she keep me on at the agency."

Nick considered this. He recalled that particularly contentious phone call to Jo-Ann while still on the plane at JFK. He'd very nearly bullied the woman into promising to keep Leila on staff. As to be expected with Jo-Ann, she hadn't taken it well. He should've known that in a battle of wills, she'd win every time.

"Makes sense," he said. "So I'm really to blame."

"No." This time she grabbed his hand and held it. "Back then I really appreciated you trying to save my job. I still do, and I need you to know that."

He nodded. And since the time had come to put their hearts on the table, he had something to confess, as well. "I need you to know that I'm proud of you. Proud of what you've accomplished this past year."

The waiter returned with marinated olives and asked to take their order. When he left she said, "You've been to my office. I really didn't accomplish much."

"You could've taken a job at any old real estate agency, but you went solo. You created something, and that takes guts. I've never done that."

"Well, thanks."

She made his heart melt with a lopsided smile. And from then on the night took on a more playful bent. The champagne worked its magic. Leila mellowed and when old acquaintances stopped at their table to say hello, he introduced her as "the thorn in my side."

"I used to be the light of your life," she said.

"You used to work harder to keep me happy."

She laughed. "Get used to the new normal."

He reached under the table and stroked her bare thigh. "I don't want to."

She slapped his hand away then ignored him and focused on the dessert menu. They ordered ice cream and when later she licked whipped cream off her fingers, he ached to take those fingers in his mouth.

"What are we going to do now?" he asked.

She pointed to the all but forgotten folder tucked under her purse. "Order espresso and go over the contract."

"I thought I'd take you home with me. You'll never guess where I'm staying."

Her eyes lit up. "Tell me."

"One hint. You've been there before. Took the grand tour and everything."

"Oh, God, you're at Ten Twenty Biscayne? The very building you're being paid to sell out?"

He winced. "When you put it that way it sounds shady."

"That view in the morning must make up for everything."

"Come with me and find out."

All evening, he'd been winding her up. He knew her well enough to know she was ready to be loved right about now. Or could it just be him? He was so easily stirred by little details: that look in her eyes, the curve of her throat and the way her hand lingered on his arm when she told a story. The cave, the desk, even her kitchen counter… those encounters were merely appetizers. He was ready for a full meal, all night in his bed, her hair spread on the pillow and her dress on the floor.

"I'm ready to get out of here," he said.

Leila pushed aside her dessert plate and reached for the folder. "I don't think we should wait on this. Unless you weren't serious about hiring me."

He rested his spoon. "Okay. Let's do it."

She produced a standard contract. "This is for exclusive representation."

"I don't want to work with anyone else."

"I don't want you changing your mind and meddling. Let me be your agent."

"I'll let you be whatever you want."

She ignored his comment and pressed on. "The term is six months."

"Let's stick to a time frame we're used to. Eight weeks."

She drew her brows together. "That's outrageous. You're putting a gun to my head. What if I don't deliver?"

"You will."

"You don't know that. It all depends on inventory. Who knows what's out there?"

"The short deadline pushes me to the front of the line, where I want to be. It forces you to make me your priority."

"You're my priority regardless! There's no line, and you know it."

Nick knew exactly what to say to end this pointless discussion. "Are you asking me to go easy on you?"

"Fine!" With a stroke of a pen, she amended the contract from six months to two. "Okay. Let's see. The standard commission applies."

"Leila!" he cried. "Let me sign the damn thing."

"There's one more thing to cover."

"What haven't we covered?"

She took a sip of water. "Just this. I don't sleep with my clients."

He tapped the contract. "Show me the clause that says that."

"I'm serious. No mixing business with pleasure."

"Can't we work around that rule?"

She shook her head. "Not this time. If we do this, I want to keep things friendly and professional."

"Why would you want that?"

She pressed her lips together the way she did when mulling over something important. "Because we've fallen into our old ways, and I don't want to fall any deeper."

"Would that be so bad?"

"I got sucked into your world once and it spit me out."

He folded his arms across his chest. "Then take me into yours."

She turned away, avoiding his eyes.

Since the night was about candid confession, Nick decided to go for broke. "Leila, if you're worried I'm going to leave again, don't be."

"For once I'm not worried about you or anyone," she said with a cool smile. "I'm focused on my career. My mentor taught me that."

Nick closed his eyes. The world had gone red. Any swell of hope he'd had in the morning had died down.

"We need a hiatus, Nick."

He didn't remind her that they'd just come out of a hiatus. A long one.

"How long are we talking about?"

"For the life of the contract. After that we'll see."

"Is that why you were pushing for six months?"

"That's a separate issue."

"How are you drawing these lines exactly?"

Her eyes pleaded with him. "Why not trust me on this?"

Nick was done arguing. He reached for the pen. "Where do I sign?"

She let out a sigh of relief and flipped to the last page. Relief. To be done with him.

Chapter 25

One week into their agreement and Leila was wondering why she'd signed on for another eight-week misadventure with Nick—as if the last one had ended so well. Nick was not the same since he'd signed the contract. His attitude had changed. No flirting. No joking. No cajoling. He didn't show up with coffee. He didn't call. To be fair, that's what she'd asked. All she'd wanted was to pump the breaks a little, to avoid barreling over a steep emotional cliff. It was too late to go back and renegotiate. And he'd signed the contract, which meant she had a job to do.

Nostalgia brought her back to where it all began, the Venetian Islands. She systematically visited each condo building, ruling out the dated ones in favor of newer construction. Narrowing her search even more, she considered properties that offered dock space and indoor parking for the Maserati. It wasn't enough for a condo to be accessible and attractive. It also had to reflect Nick's growth as a professional, his standing in the world today.

But this didn't stop her from visiting his former building and asking to tour a unit, similar to his old one, that was sitting on the market. The agent opened the door and Leila's inner scaffolding collapsed. She could not distinguish the present from the past. She wandered through the light-filled rooms, from the bedroom where she and Nick had first made love to the terrace where they'd shared breakfast the morning after. The listing agent stepped out to the hall to take a call and, to Leila's surprise, she started weeping. Back then they'd had a chance. Today she wasn't sure. Sofia had summed it up best. Breaking up is hard to do, getting back to together is nearly impossible.

* * *

Leila lined up three condos to show him and, on a sunny Tuesday morning, they met at a café. She'd intended to go over the pros and cons of each property. Nick wasn't a gullible first-time buyer and likely wouldn't make a decision based on impulse or emotion. Before she could launch into her rehearsed preamble, he reached over and absently toyed with the leather strap of her watch. It was a familiar gesture that worked to break the ice. They hadn't seen each other in days. He looked sleep-deprived. His voice was husky and the lines at the corners of his eyes had deepened, making him sexier. No fair.

"How are you?" he asked.

His fingers brushed her skin. Her pulse skipped.

"Great. And you?"

He shrugged. "Okay."

She couldn't sit still. "Maybe we should just go and—"

"Let's do it."

He was uncharacteristically quiet during the tour. Leila rattled off data like a wind-up doll: square footage, price per square-footage, number of days on the market, amenities, homeowners' association fees. Nick didn't ask any questions. Something was wrong, but she didn't dare ask. When they came to the last condo, a bit small but with a wraparound terrace that offered spectacular water views, she fell quiet, too.

"Why did you pick this neighborhood?" he asked finally.

Leila froze. "Because…you love it here."

They were in the kitchen, the width of a counter between them.

"I used to, sure."

"You don't anymore?"

"I want to start over."

What were they even talking about?

"I'll research some other neighborhoods then."

He rested his elbows on the counter and leaned close. "I know why you picked this one even though you won't admit it."

"I loved it here, too," Leila said defiantly. She wasn't afraid to admit it.

Nick's phone chimed. He turned away to read and respond to a text message. Then he showed her a photo that he'd received. "Look. My mom sent this."

It was a picture of an older man with silver hair and vivid blue eyes behind rimless glasses.

"Oh my God! Is that your father?"

Nick gave her a half smile. "He dyed his hair silver. I mean he'd gone gray. But mom says he went out, bought a kit and dyed it silver. I didn't think the man had a vain bone in his body."

"Whereas you have two hundred and six."

He pocketed the phone. "A man ought to look good. Don't you think?"

Nick favored his father. Judging by the photo, he'd look good for decades to come.

"I think you'd like my parents," he said.

Leila straightened up. "I'm sure I would."

To avoid any more talk about meeting his parents, she proposed they meet again in a week. "I've got a lot of work to do."

The following week they met in the lobby of Ocean Towers on Collins. The building's architecture was retro to a fault, paying homage to old school Vegas glam. But the waterfront location allowed direct ocean access.

Nick was a little late. And when he showed up fresh shaven and hair freshly cut, he looked so good it hurt. But she'd come prepared, too, having spent as much time on her appearance as her presentation—this building offered two vacant units for him to consider and she knew the specs by heart.

She stood to greet him and buttoned her tailored white blazer. "Good morning."

He rested a hand on her waist and, chastely, kissed her cheek. "How are you?"

"I'm excited to show you some options today."

She led him to the elevators. Even though the tight cabin smelled like smoke, she couldn't help but think of the fun they used to have in elevators. Nick turned to her and asked, "But how are *you*?"

Honestly? She'd had a rough week, knowing he was only a phone call away. And now his brief touch and kiss had sent heat through her body, kindling the dry wood of frustration.

She took a step back and leaned against the elevator wall. "I'm fine."

Something flickered in Nick's eyes. That unmistakable look of hunger.

The elevator stopped abruptly and opened onto the eleventh floor. Leila charged out and led him down the hall. The unit was well over sixteen hundred square feet, which was large by South Beach standards. There were three bedrooms and two baths. The floors were of the same veiny marble featured in the lobby, but at least the walls weren't mirrored.

Nick followed her into the master bedroom where she pointed out the closets.

The master bath was a disaster with that awful marble tile climbing up the walls. "It needs updating," Leila said nervously. "But remember, you're buying the space."

Nick pointed to the large oval tub. "I could have a party in that."

She gave him a hard stare. "Let's check out the view."

The balcony was narrow and basically useless except

maybe for a quick smoke. The view, however, was special. On that unusually sunny morning in March, the beach was pristine. Turquoise waters spread out to the horizon.

Nick asked what year the building was built.

"Nineteen seventy-one," she said. "True, it's dated. But you won't get this much space with new construction."

"What are they asking?"

"Six hundred and fifty thousand. We can negotiate something more reasonable."

"How much to renovate?"

She hadn't thought about it. "I'm guessing twenty-five grand."

"We're talking a new kitchen, total bathroom overhauls, new floors…"

"Okay," she said hotly. "I get your point. It would cost too much."

He studied her for a second. "Leila, we're just talking."

The look in his eyes was so gentle. Why couldn't she keep it together?

"It's not worth the expense," he said.

"I understand."

"And, to be honest, I don't think I'm interested in condos. Not anymore."

"Wait. You want to look at houses? Waterfront houses? Can you afford—?" She stopped herself. It wasn't her job to question his choices.

"When you think about the future, where do you see yourself? In a glorified apartment?"

"Depends on what you mean when you say 'future.' The foreseeable future or what?"

Leila refused to read too much into Nick's sudden return. He'd told her not to worry about him leaving, but she remained convinced that once a lucrative opportunity rolled in, he'd roll out—like the stone he was.

"I mean forever."

She let out a bitter laugh. "Come on, Nick."

"What's so funny? My parents have been living in the same house for the last thirty years."

"But you're nothing like them. Remember?"

"Find me a house. We'll find out."

She found him a house.

On four o'clock that Friday, three weeks into their contract, they met at a gated community on the Miami River, an area Nick had never considered. She waited in her little Mazda parked curbside and when he pulled up next to her, she pointed to the modern gate and mouthed, "Follow me."

She should know he'd follow her anywhere.

The gates parted, revealing an oasis of open space and mature trees. Nick liked what he was seeing so far. An enclave with ten to twelve newly constructed modern homes, some on the bank of the river, others on dry lots.

Leila pulled up to a remote house surrounded by tall palms. She got out of her car, her dark hair spilling over her shoulders. She wore a light camisole top and a fitted skirt that looked more like bondage. Most women wouldn't dress that way for a work engagement, but most women weren't his Leila.

Nick got out of his car and responded to her shy smile with, "Is this how you dress to meet all the clients you're not sleeping with?"

Her expression turned sour. "Yes. I would think a man like you could handle it."

"You overestimate what I can handle."

Locked in stubborn silence, she challenged him. *Why are you being a jerk?*

He apologized. "It's been a long week."

"Well, I hope this house lifts your spirits."

He looked up at the smart two-story modern house.

It was painted cream with large bay windows and exotic wood accent panels. "What do we have here?"

She smiled, seemingly encouraged. "I know when you said you wanted a waterfront home you meant the beach, but I think you should give this a chance. The neighborhood isn't exactly residential—"

"You can say that again." Seafood markets lined the narrow road that snaked along the river.

"Still, it has its charm."

"Agreed."

"It's close to downtown and Brickell, and you can hop on the causeway to get to the beach in minutes." She talked smoothly, betraying hours of rehearsal. "Should we go inside?"

"After you."

Leila headed up the stairs leading to the wide front door. He trailed her to get a look at her from behind. Before opening the door she said proudly, "This house comes with a dock."

The front door opened to a carefully staged room, contemporary in style but comfortable. The open layout was made more so by a wall of windows that showcased the yard, a modest pool—at least by his standards—and a view of the empty dock where his next big purchase would likely fit nicely. Leila directed his attention to the kitchen, as any good agent would. He appreciated the overall look—white cabinetry and glass subway tile—but thought it lacked space.

"It's small," he said disapprovingly.

"Compact." She pointed out the top-of-the-line appliances. "Two ovens, a stovetop, and look at the size of that refrigerator."

"It's small," he repeated.

"You don't even cook!" she cried.

"Consider the resale value. Size matters."

He headed out the back door to check the yard. He could picture Sunday mornings on the teak deck. He could see his new catamaran tethered to the dock. More importantly, he could picture Leila in a bikini—out of a bikini—by the pool.

"Do you like it?" she asked.

He turned to face her. She looked as if she were holding her breath. When was the last time he'd kissed her? "Let's check out the second floor."

On their way up the winding stairs, he asked for the specs.

"Brand-spanking-new construction."

"I figured." The last condo building she'd shown him was so dated he'd thought he'd seen the ghost of Frank Sinatra in the lobby.

"Three thousand square feet. On our way out, I'll show you the garage."

"How many bedrooms?"

"Four—and three and a half baths."

They'd reached the door of the master bedroom. He took in the dark wood floors, king-size bed and a sitting area set up with a flat-screen TV. "You know this kind of reminds me—" He stopped himself from saying anything more, but the look on Leila's face made it clear she'd read his mind. It reminded him of the hotel suite in New York where they'd had the time of their lives. She turned away, flustered, and led him to the en suite bath.

He found nothing offensive there. He wasn't a fan of the square sinks, but he loved the steam shower. He counted four showerheads. After a workout, it would feel good. And if Leila joined him, it would feel like heaven.

"Now let's check out the closet," she said.

The walk-in closet finishes were cheap—big-box, closet-kit stuff.

"There's plenty of room for your suits." She opened a

cabinet fitted with a safe. "Your watches could go in here. What do you think?"

Nick was touched by the effort she'd put in to finding him a home tailored to his needs. He took a step toward her. She jumped back and bumped into a shoe rack.

"If I'm off the mark, just say so," she said nervously. "Only, I don't know what the mark is. So you can't blame me if I can't hit it."

He took another step. He was close enough to kiss her. Leila looked away, her breathing erratic, and he hadn't even touched her.

"Listen," she said, "I don't know what you're trying to prove."

He studied her unhurriedly, watching the flutter of her lashes. "I think you do."

He backed off and waited outside the closet door, giving her a few minutes to collect herself.

When she joined him, she avoided eye contact and asked in a strained voice if he wanted to see the other bedrooms.

The smallest bedroom was fitted with bunk beds. Nick groaned at the sight of them. "My brother and I slept in one of those. He got the top bunk."

Leila swiveled around to face him. She looked utterly stunned. "You have a brother?"

"I'm sure I've mentioned him before."

"Never." Her tone was accusatory.

"I wasn't trying to hide him, if that's what you're thinking. He's my half brother and ten years older than me."

Leila pulled the chair from the child-size desk and sat down. "Were you two close?"

"He went off to college and we barely saw each other after that."

She studied him wide-eyed until he grew uncomfortable under her scrutiny. Then she turned to the bunk beds as if trying to imagine him and his brother, Logan, on them.

"You said your dad bought you pet fish so you wouldn't be alone, yet you had a brother."

The memory of the night he'd shared that story brought a wistful smile to his face. "He got me the fish after Logan left for school."

"You must have been seven or eight when he went away."

It wasn't a question so he didn't answer. In his mind's eye he saw Logan grinning at him through the window of their dad's truck. He'd lowered to the ground, fisted some snow into a ball and threw it just as the truck pulled away.

Leila was looking at him now with such affection he was disarmed. "I'll put an offer on this house."

"This one? Are you sure?"

It was as good as any. "I'm sure."

She stood and looked uncertain as to what her next move should be. After a moment's hesitation, she said, "Nick, I can show you more options. You don't have to settle."

He shook his head. "I'm not settling, Leila. I've always known what I wanted."

Chapter 26

One rainy morning Leila finally met with the nursing home director to finalize her aunt's transfer to hospice care. On the long drive home, she fell into a dark mood. When Leila lost her mother, her aunt had not sought to replace her and Leila had appreciated it. But her presence had always been reassuring, and now to lose her, too. *I'm grown. I can handle it.* She repeated this over and over, willing herself to believe it.

When she got back Brie was at her desk, printing out a research paper. She followed Leila into her office.

"How's auntie?"

Leila grunted a response. If she opened her mouth, she'd cry.

"That bad? Well, I have something to take your mind off of it." She handed her a sticky note with a name and a number. "An inquiry. And by the sound of him, he's almost as dreamy as Nicolas Adrian."

Nick. She'd submitted his offer, a low-ball offer, on the house. However, the seller was honeymooning in Greece. They were promised an answer in ten days. Since then, there hadn't been a reason to call or an excuse to meet. Some days she hoped he'd call anyway, but he never did. If this was the new normal that she'd been working toward, she had to admit it was pretty dull.

Leila put Nick out of her mind, returning her attention to the sticky note. As it turned out, Miller was the gift that kept on giving. He'd referred a lawyer friend with a rental property he was eager to unload. They met for lunch the next day. His name was Stephen Green. Thin, tall, with dark brown skin and equally dark brown eyes, he was handsome. As dreamy as Nick? Sure. Maybe.

Leila sat across from him at the Miracle Mile sidewalk

café, frustrated that her first thought had been to compare him to Nick. Over a glass of wine, she asked him about the property he was looking to sell.

"It's a solid house, built in the '60s. And not far from Sunset Drive."

"Great location."

Stephen said he'd bought it during the market boom, hoping to flip it. His friends had made fast money that way. But then, as his luck would have it, the renovations stalled and the market went bust.

"I couldn't give it away." He'd rented it out and started his second career as a landlord. Since the market was looking up, he figured it was time to sell.

Leila dipped a piece of bread into a shallow bowl of olive oil. "I agree."

"Miller said you knew your stuff. I'll leave pricing up to you. Obviously, I'd like to break even."

"I think we can do better than that."

The unexpected endorsement from Miller was a tremendous boost. Her self-esteem was flying high, a bouncy red balloon, and then suddenly it burst. Nick and a woman stepped out of a shop two doors down. Leila recognized Sandra Villanueva immediately.

Sandra spotted them first. She grabbed Nick's arm. "Oh, look who's here!"

Nick's gaze fell on her. Leila looked away. The last thing she wanted was a big, messy scene in front of a potential client. But her worries were unfounded. After a polite hello, Nick turned his attention to Stephen. Apparently they went way back. And now a sort of reunion was under way.

Stephen jumped to his feet and shook Nick's hand. "Hey, man. I didn't know you were back. When will you come around to the gym?"

"Soon. I miss it."

Stephen slapped him on the back. "Cool."

"We don't mean to interrupt your lunch," Sandra said. "We're on our way to meet a buyer."

"We're here on business, too," Leila said.

Instead of addressing her, Nick turned to Stephen. "Are you in the market?"

"Trying to unload a house I wanted to flip years ago," Stephen replied. "I would've called you if I'd known you were back."

"Don't worry about it," Nick said. "Leila is one of the best."

"I don't think we'll have trouble selling the house," Leila said. "It's a great investment property or first home."

"I know people who deal with developers all day," Nick said. "I can bring someone by when you're ready to show."

"Thanks. I'll give you a call. Same number?"

"The same."

"Enjoy your lunch," Sandra said.

Nick said goodbye, addressing no one in particular. Together he and Sandra drifted away, unhurried, heads together, co-conspirators. Leila gripped the butter knife like a sabre. What do you know! He'd wasted no time finding a new Monica.

The South Miami house was a modest A-frame with a cheery, yellow-shingled façade. At two hundred and fifty thousand, it was priced right. Leila enlisted Sofia to help with the open house. She showed up early to set up a wine bar and a buffet of bite-size delights. They had a solid turnout around lunchtime. After two hours, Leila was ready to lock up when an agent showed up with a special client: her old roommate Alicia.

Alicia had changed. Gone were the graduate student braids and sweatpants. Her wavy hair was pulled up in an elegant French twist and her lips and nails were painted burgundy.

"I never thought I'd see you again," Alicia said.

Leila owed her an apology and was grateful for the chance to deliver it in person. She asked Alicia's agent for a moment alone with her client.

"It's okay," Alicia said. "She's an old friend."

Once her agent was out of earshot, she dropped her Coach bag on the wood floor, ready to rumble. "Do you have something to say to me?"

"I'm sorry," Leila said quietly.

"That's a start," Alicia said. "But I want an explanation. What the hell *happened* to you?"

"I had to leave town in a hurry. Don't take it personally."

"When your roommate bails on you without notice, it's tough to not take it personally."

"It's a long story, but I lost my job and my boyfriend all on the same day."

"It looks like you've recovered both," Alicia said dryly. She pointed out the window.

Leila glanced over her shoulder. Nick was on the porch, laughing and chatting with Alicia's agent. He was with his old "friend" Marisol. *Ugh!* But wait—

"How do you know Nick?"

"He came around looking for you."

"When was this?"

"A couple of weeks after you went missing in action. I'll *never* forget it. He was waiting by the door. Scared the crap out of me."

When Nick had said he'd come looking for her, she'd imagined he'd flown down and made some inquiries at the office before hopping on the last plane back to New York. He'd never been to her apartment, and she didn't think he'd take the time to find it.

So he *had* "gone crazy" looking for her. Leila processed

the news with equal parts delight and dismay. The whole knight-in-shining-armor thing was plenty delightful. But she was dismayed with herself for having put him in that position in the first place.

"I guess it all worked out," Alicia said.

"We're not together. It's complicated."

"Why can't anything be simple these days?"

Leila glanced at Nick again. He'd slipped off his sunglasses, working his magic to charm the two women, his blue eyes expressive and alive.

But he'd come after her. Sat waiting outside her door.

"What's the deal with this house?" Alicia asked.

"What do you want to know?" Leila kept her eyes on Nick. He rested a hand on Marisol's shoulder and pretty much ate up all the good will Alicia's news had inspired.

"Hello!" Alicia cried.

Leila tore away from the window. "Sorry. That was rude."

"Yes, it was. I'm into this place. I work at the hospital and it's a short commute from here. I've been outbid several times on other houses. Anything you can tell me would help."

"All I can say is that my client really wants to sell. Put in a strong offer and I'll take it from there."

That evening Leila received two offers: one from Alicia and another slightly more competitive one from a buyer represented by Marisol. Leila got on the phone with Alicia's agent. "Could she come up a bit? We have another offer on the table."

"How much?"

"I can't tell you that, but it's solid."

Alicia pulled through, raising her offer to just above full asking plus the promise of a short escrow. It was enough to grab Stephen's attention.

"I'll take it," he said over the phone. "We've got a deal."

"Congratulations, Stephen," Leila said. "You're a land-lord no more."

"And you're a rock star," he said. "That was fast work. Miller was right about you. I'll spread the word."

Leila felt like a rock star, too. She'd done well by her client, helped out an old friend and given Marisol the fin-ger all with one transaction. Most importantly, she'd done it all on her own.

Chapter 27

Once off the phone with Stephen, Leila couldn't sit still. She was in the mood to celebrate, and it was all she could do to keep from calling Nick to share the news. By nightfall, she just couldn't take it anymore. She called Sofia.

"Hey," she said a bit aggressively. "Let's go out and have fun."

"I'm *already* out," Sofia replied. "Top of Hotel M. Come and join us."

Sofia and her girlfriends had reserved a rooftop poolside cabana, which doubled as a VIP lounge come sunset. The occasion: a girls' night out/birthday party. But Sofia chastised Leila for even needing a reason to party. "You forget the first commandment of business—work hard, play hard." She handed Leila a cocktail glass. "We're drinking Miami Highs."

Leila took a long sip, all the while reaching for her iPhone to check for missed calls.

Sofia caught her. "Are you *still* working?"

"I sold a house today. Sometimes there are follow up questions."

"Forget that. I want updates on the Nick and Leila *telenovela*."

With so many twists and turns, their story did qualify as melodrama. "I don't want to talk about it."

"Who are you kidding? You're dying to talk about it."

Sofia led her away from her pack of friends. They found a bar height table and ordered jalapeño guacamole and chips.

Leila found that she really was dying to talk about it. It had all been bottled up for so long and none of it made sense anymore. She started with her proposed moratorium on sex. "You know, to clear the slate."

"When does that ever work?" Sofia asked.

Leila admitted that it had worked a little too well to her liking.

"Got to give it to Nick, that's a boss move," Sofia said. "You asked for it, you got it."

"Now there's so much awkwardness between us."

"What did you think would happen?"

"I thought we'd get to know each other better."

Sofia wasn't buying it. "Oh, please. Leila."

"Please. What?"

"You know each other plenty."

"Not true," Leila said. "I just found out he has a brother. All this time and he never mentioned a brother."

"Okay, so you don't know his family tree," Sofia conceded. "But you know the man."

Leila loaded a pita chip with guacamole and considered this.

"Or maybe you don't," Sofia said.

Leila dropped the chip. "How do you mean?"

"I keep thinking about how you disappeared on him."

"We've been through this—"

"I know your reasons," Sofia said, "but it's not the sort of thing you do when you know somebody's heart."

Those words hit Leila so hard she felt dizzy. The other day Nick had said jokingly that she overestimated what he could handle. What if he hadn't been joking?

"I'm curious," Sofia said. "When you proposed this sex moratorium did you say, 'Let's slow down and get to know each other better.' Or did you just kick him out of bed?"

Sofia laughed at her own wit, but Leila wasn't amused. "I'm glad you're having fun."

"Want to know what I think?" Sofia asked.

"Don't stop now. You're on a roll."

"You're scared."

Leila wiped guacamole off her fingers with a napkin.

Sofia was wrong. She wasn't scared. She was flat-out terrified. What if she allowed herself to love Nick as fully and deeply as before only to lose him again? Sofia and Nick might argue that she hadn't lost him. That she'd chosen to end things. And on that point they wouldn't be wrong. But Leila knew this: when Nick's life imploded he recovered nicely with a high profile job and a fabulous new car. That wasn't how things typically worked out for her. So, maybe a little less concern for Nick, and a little more regard for her welfare were in order here.

"Hey. Were you meeting him here tonight?"

"No. Why?"

"Because if I'm not mistaken, that's him at the bar."

"What?" Leila swiveled in her seat.

Sure enough, there was Nick in heated debate with a stunning woman with jet-black hair and cocoa brown skin. She wore a mini-dress that showed off her long, shapely legs. It didn't help that Nick looked devastatingly gorgeous in one of his favorite indigo-blue shirts, sleeves rolled up, exposing tan arms. Leila floated to her feet. If he'd been seeing other women after all that talk about finding a home and being sure of what he wanted, if that was the real reason he hadn't called, she was going to toss him off this rooftop.

"What are you doing? Sit down!" Sofia whispered frantically. "For all we know she's a client."

"No, I don't think so."

"How can you be sure?"

"He has a type."

Leila took off, her heels digging into the faux grass rooftop landscape. Sofia trotted after her, carrying the purse she'd left behind.

Nick caught sight of her. His face immediately darkened with anger. *He* was mad at *her*? Really?

He stepped away from the woman and greeted her with

a tight smile. "So you do find time for fun while focusing on your career. I wouldn't have known."

"And you find time for all sorts of things while *pretending* to be heartbroken."

Nick's companion spoke up with a smooth and authoritative voice. "Excuse me. Can't you see you're interrupting?"

Whoa! Leila whirled around, prepared to launch a verbal assault when Nick draped an arm around her waist and pinned her to him.

"Christine, this is my girlfriend, Leila."

Leila fell quiet. Sofia let out a low whistle. Christine turned beet-red.

Taking advantage of the awkward silence, Sofia said hello to Nick. "Good to have you back."

"Nice seeing you, Sofia," Nick said. "How have you been?"

"Nick!" Christine snapped.

Everyone turned to Nick. In this highly volatile game, it was his turn to serve.

"Christine, please excuse us." He pulled Leila aside. They found a quiet spot at the balcony rail and stood side by side, facing the night.

"I'm not your girlfriend," Leila said flatly.

"In that case, you don't get to *pretend* you're jealous."

Leila felt heat rise to her cheeks. She stubbornly kept her eyes on the view.

"Don't you trust me?" he asked.

"I don't know that I do."

"Okay. Ask me anything."

"Who is she?"

"Someone I used to work with in New York."

"And we both know what that means," Leila said. She paused to give him time to deny the accusation, but he didn't. "What's she doing here?"

"She's in town for a convention. She called, wanted to meet."

"What does she want?"

"What do you think?"

His straightforward answers were unnerving. She wanted so badly to catch him in a lie, to watch him squirm.

"She's in love with you."

Leila stated the fact to better accept it. In her warped mind, loving Nicolas Adrian was her personal privilege. Who was this Christine person? Why hadn't he ever mentioned her? What had he done or said to make her want to follow him from Manhattan to Miami?

Nick's tone softened. "No, she's not."

"Yes, she is. I know what it looks like."

"Leila, she doesn't even know me, not really."

Sofia approached and suggested that one or both of them consider making alternate plans for the evening. "This rooftop ain't big enough for all of us."

"I'm tired," Leila said. "I'm going home."

"I'll come over after I'm done."

"After you're done with your date?" Leila asked. "Don't even think about it."

Chapter 28

It was the fitting end of a horrible day. All Nick could make of it was the "universe" Leila carried on about was screwing with him.

It had all started at eight in the morning. An unscheduled meeting with Reyes had culminated in a shouting match. Reyes was frustrated that his ground-floor units weren't moving fast enough. But the simple truth was that they were priced too high. Nick couldn't get the stubborn old man to admit it. No one in his or her right mind would fork out one grand per square foot for an eye-level view of pedestrian traffic. "Buyers aren't that dumb. Not anymore."

Reyes had scoffed at him. "We offer the best amenities."

"Who gives a damn about amenities?" Nick had asked. "No one stays home long enough to enjoy them."

During the meeting he had two missed calls, both from Christine. He was considering blocking her when the phone rang in his palm. Frustrated, he answered.

She wasted no time. "I'm in town, and I want to see you."

"Not going to happen. I'm busy working."

"This is about work. I'm in town for a convention, but I may have a client for you. Ten Twenty Biscayne. Right?"

Nick had the distinct feeling of walking into a trap. "Right."

"Meet me for dinner and we'll discuss it."

"I'll meet you for a drink. Where are you staying?"

That had led to this: him parked in the alley behind Leila's car, next to the dumpster. Texting her and hoping she'd let him in.

I'm outside. Give me five minutes.

By the time he'd made it to the front door, her key was turning in the dead-bolt lock. The door gave way and she greeted him with icy silence. She looked oddly sexy, her tiny frame overwhelmed by an oversized T-shirt, her hair in a messy ponytail.

"I was asleep," she said finally.

"No, you weren't." He moved past her and looked around for a place for them to sit and talk. There was no couch in the front room; Brie's desk took up most of the space. He wondered how she could live this way.

"I told you not to come."

"You and I need to talk."

"What about? Your crazy ex-girlfriend wants you back. And?"

Nick tried not to smile. "She's not *crazy*. She's actually very sharp."

"But she was your girlfriend?"

"We weren't together, Leila. You saw to that."

"I'm starting to think it was for the best."

He pulled out a chair and got settled for the long haul. "I'm not mad about this. At least I get to see a glimpse of *my* Leila."

She planted herself before him. "If that's what you're pining for, Nick, forget it. That's over."

"What's over?" The hem of her T-shirt didn't clear the top of the thighs. He traced the line with a finger.

She jerked away, coming dangerously close to kneeing him in the groin. It only made him laugh. "Leila, you don't get it both ways. Do you want me or don't you?"

"Everybody wants you, Nick. Remember?"

"What does that mean?"

She turned away. He got up and walked around her. "What does that mean?"

Leila's face was ravaged. Nick wanted only to hold her and take away that pain. But she wouldn't let him touch her.

"It means Connie Madison can't be without you, and Reyes loves you like a son," she said. "That's not my life. People don't shower me with love. And I lose everyone I love."

"Not me," Nick said. "You haven't lost me. I'm here. But if you can't see that, I don't know what else to do."

"Don't do anything. Just go."

Nick rose to his feet. She stepped back and walked around Brie's desk.

"Did I tell you about those first months in New York?" he asked. "I never slept, waited weeks for you to reach out to me. Finally, I got your address from HR and flew back so we could talk. But there was no talking to you then, either. You were gone. Being on good terms with Connie Madison and Raul Reyes makes up for all that. Right?" His tone sarcastic.

Leila was stooped over the desk. Nick waited a long while for her to meet his eyes before he gave up and walked out. He stood outside her door long after she'd locked it. More and more he felt as if he were building towers in the sand, the high tide wiping away any progress he made, him tirelessly starting over every time.

Next morning Leila woke with her heart trapped in ice. What had gotten into her last night? *You saw Nick with that beautiful woman and you lost your mind, that's what.*

Rightly or wrongly, Leila was hotly, insanely jealous. Nick had always made her feel as if she was the only woman in the world for him. Now this Christine person challenged that. Petty jealousy had popped the cork, and every other foul emotion bottled inside her had spilled out.

Brie wasn't scheduled to come in. Leila was glad to have her home to herself. She needed time alone. No hunting for clients. No networking. No hustling of any kind. She had to sort herself out. The way Nick had looked at her before he left. This time she couldn't pretend it was unmerited.

Leila found her sneakers buried deep in her closet and went out for a run. When she returned, she used an app to meditate for a full half-hour. She was determined to do the things that used to keep her sane. Before she became consumed with proving her self-worth to Jo-Ann Wallace and other people who didn't matter, she'd had a balanced emotional life. She was determined to find her way back to the woman Nick had fallen in love with and had not wanted to let go. It didn't matter if they had a future together or not. She never again wanted to see that look of disappointment in his eyes.

However, Leila's newfound Zen was shattered late in the afternoon. The developer's agent called with a response to Nick's offer on the Miami River house. Her name was Claire, and she was never anything but sunny.

"Unfortunately, Leila, I have bad news. The offer was rejected."

"Any counter?"

"Nope. My client's really insulted, to be frank."

Nick's offer on the house was roughly one hundred grand below asking price. Leila had warned him not to go about it so aggressively, but he hadn't listened. Still, the outright rejection was equally insulting.

"The neighborhood doesn't command the asking price," Leila said.

"My guy is standing firm," Claire said. "Talk to your client. I'd love it if we could come to a deal."

And so the time for soulful meditation had come to an end. She had to contact Nick and come up with a new action plan. Before she did any of that, she had to apologize for last night's outburst. She was intent on doing it in person.

Leila showered and dressed. She was looking for her keys when the doorbell rang. Certain it was Nick, she raced to the door. The apology she'd rehearsed in the shower was at the tip of her tongue. She yanked the door open.

It wasn't Nick.

Leila greeted her unexpected visitor with a cold, polite smile.

Christine was in an aqua-blue romper and heels. She wore too much bronzer, as women tended to do while vacationing in Miami. But she was poised and calm. Leila debated whether to invite her into her office. What was the point in that? They stood facing each other in the cavernous front room.

In the hostile silence that locked them in place, Leila understood one thing clearly: her jealousy had nothing to do with Christine's looks or her history with Nick. Christine had guts, which she sorely lacked. Crazy or not, she'd booked the flight, hopped on the plane and hunted down her man. Christine had dared to do the one thing that Leila hadn't. So Leila thanked the universe for the gift of Christine.

Christine was saying something and Leila strained to pay attention.

"I hope you don't mind. I looked you up online and decided to stop by your…agency. Or whatever this is."

"I do mind, actually."

"I won't be long," she said. "I'm on my way to the airport. The taxi is waiting, meter running."

"I suggest you get to it."

Christine nodded. "He dropped everything to move back here. I can't believe it was all for you."

"No, no, no." Leila was happy to set her straight on that point. "He'd landed the sort of work that always interested him, I think. And if we hadn't run into each other at a party—" Aware she was oversharing, Leila stopped talking midsentence.

"That's not how he tells it," Christine said.

"Really? What did he say?"

"If you think I'm here to patch things up between you two—"

This was going nowhere. "Why are you here?"

"I want to know what the deal is," Christine said. "Nick's a dreamer. He might've come here hoping to find something he'd lost, but last night opened my eyes. You two are not in sync. If things aren't going to work out, please tell me."

Leila felt a flash of anger. She was not about to hand deliver Nick to this woman who, truly, didn't know the first thing about him. He wasn't some starry-eyed dreamer. He set goals and met them.

"We may have some things to work out," Leila said, "but Nick and I are connected. You're here because you know it."

"Let me tell you something you may not know," Christine said. "Nick will wake up sooner or later. He'll see you, this mom-and-pop shop you're running and this city for the joke that it is. It's all fun-in-the-sun now, but it won't last. He's going to need more."

"Are we done?" Leila asked.

"I think so."

Leila escorted Christine out, locked her door and stood staring at it in a rage. Was it true that she and Nick were no longer in sync? Was it obvious to everyone? Of all the things Christine had said, that was the one thing that bothered her most. Bothered and scared her. If it was true, she couldn't let it go on.

Chapter 29

Nick poured himself some whiskey, then poured it into the kitchen sink. He was facing another sleepless night and the liquor wouldn't help. He paced the living room floor, tossing his phone from one hand to the other as if it were on fire. Every night it was the same struggle: wanting to call her, but needing her to realize she wants him, too. After last night, he thought it best to give her time to cool down. He stopped at the windows, taking in the night view. Across the street, the lights of the Intercontinental Hotel stained the darkened sky.

I'm losing her.

One thing was sure. Nothing would come from sitting at home waiting for Leila to come around. She could yell at him, she could kick him out, but he had to try something. He had to fight. He pocketed his phone, grabbed his keys and headed for the door, pausing to check the time. Eight o'clock. He considered ordering dinner. Leila would never turn away good food. Then the phone rang and the doorman announced Leila Amis was in the lobby to see him. Nick leaned against the wall and laughed for the first time that day, surprising the younger man on the phone.

"What should I do?"

"Send her up."

He waited out in the hall, his blood running warm. Although the circumstances looked good, he refused to read too much into it. Lately, her behavior had been so erratic it would be dumb to draw any conclusions. But when she stepped off the elevator in the littlest of little black dresses, he felt the winds blowing in his favor.

"I have bad news," she said softly.

"Yes?"

"Your offer was flat-out rejected," she said. "No counter."

"You came all this way to tell me that?"

"I like to deliver bad news in person."

"Okay, well." He shrugged. "Bummer."

"Aren't you upset?"

"Not really."

"We're talking about your future home!"

"A—I'm aware of that. B—I'm cautious about what I call mine these days."

"Are you going to revise your offer?"

"I'll have to sleep on it."

She looked around, as if searching for something more to add.

"Are you sure that's all you came to say?"

She shifted her weight from one foot to another, but stayed quiet.

"I'd hate to think you lost your nerve."

"Your Christine stopped by my office just now."

Nick was sorry to hear that. Maybe Kim had been right about her all along.

"She's not my anything," he said. "What did she want?"

"She wanted to know if things were going to work out between us."

"Funny. I've been wondering about that myself."

The elevator bell chimed again, a reminder that they were having an intimate discussion in the hallway. He took her by the hand and led her into his place. Once inside he said, "It took Christine to get you here."

"It didn't," she said. "I'm here to apologize. I'm not proud of my behavior last night. It was petty, and I don't want to be that girl."

"Leila, I don't need an apology. I need you back."

She dropped her purse on the living room rug. Without a word, she slipped the dress's thin straps over her shoulders and worked the stretchy fabric to her waist, revealing the beautiful spread of black lace underneath. Nick recognized it immediately. He'd bought the bodysuit for her as a "Sorry I effed up" gift. She was wearing it now to express the same sentiment.

With a few moves of the hips, the dress fell to her feet. She looked at him, eyes vivid. "I'm back."

The tension of the past weeks broke. Nick felt light and in one swift move he swept her into his arms and laid her on the soft area rug.

She laughed, startled. "Take me upstairs!"

"I'll take you here first."

She hastily unbuttoned his shirt. "I'm in no position to argue."

He leaned in and kissed her. Her arms came around his neck and she kissed back hungrily. Nick worked feverishly to extricate her from the lace encasing. When he was done, he sat between her knees. In the darkened room, the city lights left a pattern of dots on her gorgeous skin. He had no clue how he'd managed to stay away from her for so long, not when they were in the same city.

She whispered his name

"Yes, beautiful."

"Say you love me."

"After what you put me through?"

She struggled to raise herself onto her elbows. "Nick!"

"I love you." He touched her between her legs, feeling her heat and dampness. "But I have one hundred ways to make you pay."

She raised a slender ankle to his shoulder, resting it there. "Don't disappoint me."

Nick curled a hand around her ankle and pressed his lips to it. She relaxed onto the rug and he watched her expression soften.

Yes. She was back.

Naked in Nick's kitchen, Leila felt comfortable in her skin. Take-out containers, plastic forks and long-stemmed wineglasses were scattered on the honed-granite surface. Smartly hid spotlights let out a soft, flattering glow. All in all, the condo wasn't so bad. Even the ultra-modern cabinets were growing on her.

"You know, at first I thought those red cabinets were too much, but in this light they're okay."

Nick cleared away the food, leaving only the half-full wineglasses. "I'll tell Sandra you said that."

"Why?"

"She's my landlord."

"This is Sandra's place?"

"She was one of Reyes's first buyers. It's a good investment."

She hated the idea of him living in another woman's property, even if it was only investment property. She tried to change the subject. "Can you see the sunrise from the kitchen, too?"

"How about we stay up and find out?" He stood behind her, gathering her hair, kissing a tender spot at the nape her neck. "But I don't remember you being a morning person."

"I live in a bat cave. I dream of the sun."

"You're welcome to live here."

He kissed the one spot repeatedly, until in her mind it turned fiery red. Was he serious?

"I don't think that's a good idea."

He bit her, and she cried, "Ouch!"

"Let me guess," he said, his voice gritty. "You're going to say, 'Let's take it slow.'"

She was controlled by his tiny gestures. His fingers in her hair. His kisses. She couldn't move. She could barely breathe. "Can't we do things my way for a change?"

"Your way means we split up. Every damn time."

"I wasn't trying to split us up. You took it too far this time."

"I did what you asked."

"No. You played me like a Rubik's cube."

Nick laughed. "What are you talking about?"

"You figured out all the things I like, and you took them away."

"I don't know what you mean."

He wrapped an arm around her waist and pressed her back to his chest. She felt him hard against the small of her back.

"You never called."

"Neither did you."

"You tried to make me jealous."

"Ditto."

"You never looked at me," she said between labored breaths.

"Not true." He held her tighter. With his free hand, he reached down and stroked her. She let her head fall back onto his shoulder. "But I'm confused. That's what you'd asked for."

But that wasn't what she'd wanted.

"You wanted your space, you'd made that clear. I wasn't going to crowd you." He spoke gruffly into her ear. "You can come and go..." He slipped two fingers inside her. "Right now I know you want to come."

Oh, God. Climax came swiftly, cutting her at the knees. She gripped the counter's edge, but Nick held tight. As the world spun around her, she knew that if he asked her to move in again, if he asked her to do anything at all, she'd say yes.

Thankfully her phone rang, the old-school rotary ring tone shrill and insistent.

He abruptly let her go. "Who calls you at one in the morning?"

"Let's find out," she teased.

The phone was in her purse on the living room rug. She went to get it, doing her best pageant walk—the languid walk of swimsuit competitions—knowing his eyes were on her. No one ever called this late and she fully expected a wrong number. She was shocked to see the Caller ID display. Weston Hospice.

Chapter 30

Nick drove but he wouldn't keep quiet and focus on the road, as Leila desperately wanted him to. He had a million questions. "Is this the aunt who raised you?"

"Yes."

"How long has she been sick?"

She'd found a small brush in her purse and was working it through her tangled hair with aggressive strokes. "Only a few months. The cancer had spread long before she was diagnosed. She didn't have a chance."

"And you weren't going to tell me your one living relative was dying?"

"I have other relatives. I just don't see them much."

"That's not the point."

Leila slapped the back of the tiny useless brush into her open palm. "Why are you picking a fight now?"

He reached out and stroked her arm. "Sorry. I don't mean to."

With nothing but clear roads, the drive west took under twenty minutes.

The hospice building was on the same grounds as the nursing home. Nick pulled into the medical campus and followed the signs pointing to the visitors' garage. Leila tried to stop him. "You don't have to park. Just leave me at the entrance."

"No way."

She sat gripping her purse. Despite the late hour, the garage was full. Nick parked on the third floor and took the lead heading toward the elevator. It was large enough to fit a casket and still Leila felt claustrophobic. The doors slammed shut and she began to unravel.

"Look. You can't stay. You have to go."

"You're talking crazy."

"You can't be here."

"Why not?"

How could she explain this to him? They existed in a bubble. When they were together, life was good. They made love. They made money. They had fun. It was all very glamorous and sexy. But outside that bubble was real life. *Her* life. And it was dark, depressing and nothing he was used to.

The elevator opened onto the ground floor. Nick held the doors open with an outstretched arm, waiting for a response. After an awkward pause, she gave up and stormed past him. The bright fluorescent lights and smell of bleach welcomed them into an unforgiving world.

Camille had had a heart attack, followed minutes later by another. The DNR that she'd signed only authorized medical staff to keep her comfortable. Now Leila questioned the wisdom of that plan.

"Maybe you should do that thing," she said to the doctor. "That thing on TV with the paddles."

They were huddled in the hall outside her aunt's room. The hospice doctor, a brittle-looking woman, was surprisingly soft-spoken and patient.

"Ms. Amis, we agreed to respect your aunt's wishes."

"I know, but can't we do something?"

"Even if we could, it's much too late. She is sedated and comfortable."

Nick took her hand and the gesture instantly calmed her. She kept her eyes down. For the first time she noticed the grayish color of the linoleum floor.

"Can we see her?" Nick asked.

"Yes, but keep your voices low, and be mindful of what you say. She may be able to hear you."

The doctor walked away, her Crocs making a little squeaking sound.

Nick lifted her chin with a finger. "Are you ready, honey?"

"I am, but you should go now. I'll be fine."

He squeezed her hand. "I'll only stay a minute."

The small room was bathed in soft light. Leila timidly approached the bed. Since finalizing her aunt's transfer to hospice, she'd been actively grieving her loss, determined that death wouldn't catch her off guard. But seeing Camille now, medicated and serene, finally free to relive in dreams all the adventures that had shaped her life, she felt reassured. It was time to let her go.

Leila pulled up a chair to the bedside and was startled to see Nick comfortably settled on the small couch under the window. She stated the obvious. "You're not leaving."

He silenced his phone and slipped it in his pocket. "Are you?"

"I don't want her to be alone."

"I don't want *you* to be alone."

They sat in silence while time passed.

Leila considered Nick. He was not the happy-go-lucky guy who'd left for New York over a year ago, and it was time she faced that. It had taken a while for her to notice the difference. He was more focused, calculating and determined. His self-confidence seemed more deeply rooted and his actions less impulsive, more sure. She worried that time hadn't matured her at all. She wrestled with the same issues, and frankly was tired of it.

"I'm a hater, Nick," she said quietly.

He looked at her questioningly.

"You're so damn perfect. Handsome, smart, successful—you had every advantage. I didn't think you could be hurt." She paused. "And now I know you were."

She could love him or envy him. The two emotions couldn't coexist. One would erode the other.

Even this confession didn't faze him. "Don't apologize

to me. I messed this up so many ways. You had a lot going on, and I never gave it a thought. Then I took off and left you vulnerable." After a silence he added, "I put stock in the wrong things."

This mea culpa surprised her. "No. You had to go."

"I didn't."

"And what? Lose out on your promotion? You worked hard. No one deserved it more."

"I lost you."

This was the most sincere exchange they'd ever had, but it felt like a postmortem. She had new clarity on their past, but no insight on a possible future. Where would they go from here?

The door cracked opened. A nurse entered the room, pushing a cart into the tight space. Without making too much eye contact, she checked on Camille, logging her vital signs in a chart. She wished them good night and discretely exited the room.

Nick said, "It's cold in here. Are you okay?"

She frowned and tugged on the hem of her dress. Her bare thighs were covered in goose bumps. "I look like a hooker."

He laughed quietly. "Yeah, but I like it."

Pointing to the bed, she said, "Camille would've liked it, too. She was a wild one back in the day."

"Tell me about her."

Leila wondered where to start. With the possibility of Camille overhearing them, she had to be careful. Then it came to her. "You should know she was a knockout…"

Camille passed away at six in the morning. After all the formalities were taken care of, Leila and Nick walked back to the garage hand in hand. In the same elevator in which she'd asked him to leave, she now clung to him, burying her face in his chest, ever so grateful he'd stayed.

Chapter 31

Nick was late. The funeral service was almost over when he arrived. Another heated meeting with Reyes had gone into overtime. However this time, feeling like a titan since he'd gotten Leila back, Nick had walked out, letting the old man know that he had a personal matter to attend to. And besides, he had an ace in his pocket. Christine, however furious she was with him, had referred her client: a Chinese businesswoman attracted to the building specifically for its amenities. Nick was in talks for her to purchase and combine the two remaining units.

Now he slipped into a pew near the back of the chapel and sat next to Brie. The girl leaned close and whispered, "I've never seen her this sad."

Leila looked frail in an austere black dress. He wished he could take her away for a few days, but with Reyes on his back that wouldn't be possible. Nick decided right there that it was time to free himself of the old man. Once this gig was over, he would have to move on. What that meant, though, he wasn't sure.

After the service, he joined Leila and stood by her while she thanked the handful of relatives who'd shown up. When they were alone, she complained of a headache. He drew her close, kissed her eyelids and got a taste of her tears.

"I've got to go back to work, but I'll come by tonight."

"Or I can come over," she proposed.

Nick recognized her modus operandi. She never let him anywhere near where she lived, always opting to spend time at his place. He lovingly said no. This time they were going to do things differently.

"You have a headache. Stay put, and I'll bring dinner."

She pushed away from him, and came right out with it. "Okay. But you won't stay the night."

"Why not?"

The chapel workers were busy turning off the lights, signaling it was time for them to leave. Nick took her hand and led her out to the parking lot. Only their two cars remained.

She picked up where they'd left off. "You won't be comfortable. That's all."

He had to take her to his parents' home as soon as possible to dispel the myth that he needed luxury to survive.

"Do you have hot running water?" he asked. "Because that's all I need."

"Nick, I think it would be best if—"

He kissed her. "See you tonight."

Leila drove home. Her shoes pinched her feet, and she slipped them off before heading to the kitchen to make a cup of chai tea. The funeral marked the end of an era. The family she was born into was nearly gone. After her parents died, she'd learned to rely solely on herself. Her aunt had been a comforting presence, and that was all. Frankly, that was all her aunt had wanted to be. In her own way, Leila was a rolling stone. But now Nick seemed no longer content to play the role of the feel-good boyfriend. He was elbowing his way into the dense woods of her life in such a way that she was no longer comfortable. He'd stayed with her at the hospital. Later, when she'd tried to get him to give her space to deal with relatives and set up the funeral, he'd said no. And now he wanted to spend the night at her place.

These were not outrageous demands, mind you. A normal person would have welcomed all of it. The only conclusion: she wasn't normal. She recalled a conversation they'd had while driving to the funeral home the day after Camille had passed.

"Listen," he'd said. "I've been told I'm not a team player

and I'm working on that. But if you can't rely on me even a little then you're not, either."

Brie showed up, carrying a package. "This was delivered just now. I signed for it."

It was from the nursing home. Leila guessed it contained the last of Camille's personal possessions. Although large, the box was disturbingly light. She set it aside for later.

Brie sat at her desk and started up her computer. "What's on the agenda today?"

"Nothing," Leila said. "We're closed. Remember?"

"I thought we could straighten up, shred old documents, back up our files, stuff like that."

"Or play Solitaire?" Leila proposed.

She saw right through the girl. Brie had come to keep her company. Just like Nick, she wouldn't go away.

"Sounds good," Brie said. "But I'll play Candy Crush."

Later that afternoon, Sofia came around. She dumped her massive Louis Vuitton tote onto Leila's kitchen table and pulled up a seat. "The parking sucks. Why are you living here?"

Leila poured her a cup of coffee. "The rent is cheap."

"Sometimes cheap can be taxing."

"You're telling me."

Sofia reached for her hand and, with a contrite smile, said, "If it weren't for work I'd have been there. You know that, right?"

"Of course."

Sofia had just made it back from Key Largo. She'd been hired to throw a grand opening party for a newly renovated bed-and-breakfast. Since she'd missed the funeral, she insisted on coming straight over.

"How did it go?"

"Very well." Camille had left specific orders for a simple send-off.

"When my uncle died last year, we were shocked at how pricey things were. How are you doing with money?" Sofia asked the question with none of the reservations most people felt about bringing up the taboo subject.

"My aunt had taken care of everything months ago. All I had to do was make the call, sign the paperwork and show up."

"Did anyone else show up?"

"I wasn't alone," Leila reassured her. "Some relatives flew down from New Jersey."

"Anyone else?"

"Both Brie and Nick were there."

Sofia nodded her approval. "Things good between you two?"

Leila nodded.

"What's wrong?"

"Nothing!"

Could she complain that things were a little too good? Not without getting slapped, she imagined.

"Leila, don't make me twist your arm."

"He wants to be in my life, like *all* in."

"Like all up in your business."

"Yes."

"Most women have the opposite complaint."

"I know! It's just…" Leila exhaled, a knot in her chest came undone. "To be honest, I never thought we were going to work out or have any kind of future."

"Why not?"

"Well." Leila got up from the table and rinsed out her cup. "He was the go-getter, the shark. I was the temp hired to answer his phones."

Sofia sipped her coffee. "Remember that open house in Bayshore? The one I helped you guys with? I saw you interact, and it didn't seem that way to me. You looked like a team."

That night seemed so long ago. Leila blinked the memory away.

"How are things with you?" she asked.

"Oh, you know, nothing's new. Franco proposed. I said yes. Same old, same old."

"What?" Leila rushed over to her. "When did this happen?"

"In Key Largo." Sofia showed off the princess-cut diamond on her left hand. "Midnight stroll on the beach, full moon, he gets down on one knee… You know how it goes."

"Sofia, you're going to be a bride! Heaven help us!"

Her friend let out a wicked laugh, confirming that her longtime boyfriend had effectively released the bridal equivalent of the kraken. She then pushed back her chair and hopped to her feet. "Hug me. Tell me you're happy for me."

Leila did as instructed. "I'm crazy happy for you."

When they settled back down, Leila said, "You and Franco are so normal, I can't stand it."

"Are you kidding me?" Sofia said. "We broke up so many times I lost count. Then one day I took matters into my own hands."

"Meaning what?" Knowing Sofia that could mean anything.

"I moved in with him."

"Did he ask you to?"

"Nope. I just showed up with my packed bags."

"That's not psycho at all."

"I didn't want to waste any time," Sofia said. "Sometimes, when you're sure, you have to make a move."

Chapter 32

Nick called to say he was running late. A last minute deal had come through, and he was close to selling out the building. He still planned on coming over, after heading home to pick up a few things. Leila told him not to worry about dinner. She had a solitary meal at a gourmet supermarket counter. When she got back, she took the package from the nursing home into her bedroom. She reached under her bed for her wooden box of memories.

Along with her sparkly tiara, it held a few mementos of her parents. Nothing terribly fancy: their gold wedding bands, old passports, birth certificates and photos. These simple things had the power to bring back her mother's shy smile and her father's boisterous laugh. She added Camille's Bible, old photos, a pair of diamond earrings and a tube of Revlon lipstick that her aunt had kept for no apparent reason. If only the past could be so neatly packed away.

She held her mother's wedding ring and Camille's lipstick in the palm of one hand. As a girl, she'd thought she'd had to choose between the two women, as if she could only grow up to be as serious as her mother or as frivolous as her aunt. How dumb was that? Both women had shaped her and both had left her with the burden of their unfulfilled lives.

Now what about her own life? How fulfilled was she? Leila fingered the tiara, feeling no need to put it on this time. Then she packed everything away, locked the box and rolled her head from side to side like she'd been taught in yoga class. Everything ached. From this angle, her bedroom walls looked dingy in the crisp white light of her bedside lamps. She tried sprucing the space up before Nick's arrival. She changed the sheets, tidied the room and still wasn't satisfied.

Forget this. If she packed quickly she could beat Nick to his place.

Leila had only meant to pack an overnight bag, but before she knew it half the contents of her closet was folded into a massive suitcase. She rolled it out to the back alley and shoved it into the trunk of her car. She'd come back for the rest in the morning.

Too much time had been wasted. She had to make a move.

This is what he wants, Leila told herself as she circled Nick's block. At night the downtown neighborhood lost its daytime glamour. The side streets were dark and deserted. She was weary of driving, but couldn't bring herself to pull into the building's garage. Showing up unannounced at a man's house—anyone's house—with a packed suitcase and fully stocked makeup case was a bold if not bizarre move. She had to be sure.

From the start Nick had known his mind. All he'd ever wanted was for them to be together. He'd never wavered on that point. What if she'd gone with him to New York? She could've gotten licensed there or simply gone back to school. She could've at least given it a trial run. The point was that she'd had options but had chosen not to consider them. The coward in her had held her back.

When Leila finally pulled into Nick's building, she was still nervous and unsure. She had the access code to the private garage. Relieved to see Nick's car there, she left her modest Mazda next to the mighty Maserati and wheeled her suitcase to the elevators. She hesitated to press the button. There'd be no turning back from this. She couldn't wake up in the morning and change her mind. She gripped the handle of her suitcase, tempted to wheel it back to her car, when the elevator doors slid open and a couple stepped out, hand in hand. It seemed to Leila that the universe had decided her fate.

* * *

Leila rang the doorbell and, for good measure, knocked on the door until she heard footsteps in the entryway. Nick flung the door open without bothering to ask who was there. He was all but naked except for a pair of gray boxer briefs—and, oh, my lord.

"Hey," she said, nervously.

"What are you—?" His gaze fell to the suitcase that reached up to her hip. "What's this?"

"You asked me to move in, remember?"

He stepped out into the hall and shut the door behind him as if protecting his territory from an invading tribe. Leila's heart sagged. This was not the scene she'd imagined when she'd concocted the plan. She'd pictured him carrying her across the threshold like a bride. Instead he was acting as if she were diseased.

"All this so I don't spend the night at your place?"

"No, that's not it," Leila said. "Do we have to talk about this in the hall? You're practically naked."

She managed to speak calmly, despite her growing panic.

He let her in. She wheeled the massive suitcase into the main room and left it by the couch. Then she stood, awkwardly balancing her arms. His cautious demeanor stripped her of her confidence.

"Nick, I thought this was what you wanted."

"Never mind what I want. Tell me what you want out of this."

She noticed with some alarm that he had not left the entryway. The door was ajar and he was still holding on to the knob.

"I want to be with you. If it makes you more comfortable, you can pack your things and move in with me. But I warn you, the view is better here—and so are the kitchen appliances."

"Are you sure this isn't just a reaction to losing your aunt?" he asked.

"It is, and it isn't."

Nick ran a hand through his hair. "You said my world spit you out, but you won't let me into yours. How will this work?"

"It'll work because I believe in us this time," she said. "You're right about me. I don't know how to rely on anyone but myself, and I'm so damn tired!"

Being separated from him had been devastating, and she was no longer interested in pretending that it hadn't been. It had hurt her, kept her isolated from the man who truly loved her. He released the door and let it click shut. The sound was a welcome comfort.

"You can rely on me," he said. "Only I'm not interested in quick fixes."

Why couldn't he see this for the bold romantic gesture that it was? She was taking a leap of faith, the same but somewhat shorter leap that Christine had claimed he'd made for her.

"Christine said—"

"I don't want to talk about Christine."

"She said you moved back to Miami for me. Is that true?"

"Yes."

"Be honest," she said. "You were offered a good job. You came back to work with Reyes."

"I came back to be near you, so I took a job with Reyes," Nick said firmly. "I had a job, a good one. And this new one isn't the dream you make it out to be."

"Why didn't you tell me?"

If she'd known this up front, everything could have been different.

"Tell you what? You'd moved out of the city to get away from me."

"That's not how it was."

"It's hard to see it any other way."

How could she explain? "That thing between us? It *is* relentless. After you left, it tore me apart. I wasn't thinking."

Leila, fearful she wasn't making any sense, turned away. She pressed a hand over her mouth to keep from crying out in frustration. All the emotions of the day rattled through her. What was she thinking showing up like this?

Nick rushed to take her in his arms, murmuring, "I'm sorry, love. I'm sorry."

Leila eased herself from his embrace. She wouldn't let him apologize for any of it.

"The first time you said my name I was yours. I'd have followed you anywhere, if I weren't so damn scared."

"Or if you trusted me," he said. "Do you trust me now?"

It was the right question to ask. Everything depended on it. "Yes."

He pulled her close again, kissed her hair and whispered, "Then let me love you."

Leila wrapped her arms around him and breathed him in. He was the prize.

Epilogue

One month later

Leila had a tough time coming out of the ocean with the rough waves lapping at her calves. The sand was warm under her feet. She walked up the beach toward the round lounge bed that Nick had rented for the day. He was there, stretched out on his back, thumbing his phone. Tan, eyes hidden behind Wayfarer sunglasses, and feet dusty with sand, he looked rested and content for the first time ever. Nick, her ruthless shark, her tender lover and her friend— what was he doing on his phone?

After he'd finished up his business with Reyes, they'd driven down to Miami Beach and checked in at the Tides. Five days later, they were in no hurry to check out. Their penthouse suite offered every convenience. They spent their days poolside or at the beach. Each night they strolled along Ocean Drive and picked a restaurant at random. They were doing things Nick's way, spending time together and listening to each other's stories. Leila had to admit his way of getting reacquainted was infinitely more pleasurable than her own. She didn't have to work so hard to figure him out. She knew his heart and that was more than enough.

She toweled off, and asked him to put away the phone. It was the first sign that real life was creeping back.

"I want to show you something," he said, not looking up.

Leila dropped the damp towel, wanting him to see something, too.

For a brief second he raised his eyes and his heated gaze swept over her, taking in her glistening brown skin showed off nicely in a white bikini. "Come here, you tease."

She crawled over and stretched out beside him.

"I got a lead on something that hits the market tomorrow."

"I don't care."

He shot out some buzzwords, all the while absently tracing lazy circles around her navel. "Mid-century construction. Pool. Waterfront. Dock and boatlift. Bayshore."

"Bayshore?" She sat up.

"Do I have your attention now?"

She snuggled close to him. "Remember our first house in Bayshore?"

They'd worked together to make the sale. At the time, Leila had been too ashamed of her inexperience to see it that way.

He handed her the phone and there it was, the white mid-century house surrounded by palm trees. Leila's heart swelled. They say you never forget your first.

"It's still standing. I thought the developer was going to knock it down."

"He's bankrupt. Now he's cashing out."

"What are you thinking?"

"I'm thinking that the first time I heard you laugh we were in that house. We had our first fight there. And I'll never forget the way you looked that night by the pool. We could spend our nights that way. Would you like that?"

"Nick…"

"I'll take that for a yes. Now it's up to you to get me this house. I want to lock it down before it hits the market."

She fell onto her back. "Just pick up the phone and finish the job," she said. "I don't deserve that commission."

"Oh, you deserve it."

He came to lie on top of her, pinning her arms over her head. Then he bit the tender part of her earlobe and called her his magical fairy.

Leila twisted under his weight and laughed.

"How about we work on this together?" He trailed

kisses down the length of her collarbone. "How does that sound?"

"It definitely *feels* really good."

"Give me an answer."

"Sure. It's not like I've got a lot going on."

"In that case, how about we work together from here on out?"

She laughed. "I guess as an experienced small business owner, I could mentor you, take you under my wing."

"All I want is to be under your wing."

"Are you serious?"

He hovered over her. "Very."

She looked into his eyes and caught a glimpse of their future. Swimming in the deep end of the ocean, no familiar landmarks in sight.

"What do you say?" he asked. "I could branch out on my own, but I'd rather have a partner, someone at my side. Can you be that someone?"

"Nick," she whispered, her heart taking flight, "I am that someone."

* * * * *

COMING NEXT MONTH
Available March 20, 2018

#565 STILL LOVING YOU
The Grays of Los Angeles • by Sheryl Lister

Malcolm Gray is Lauren Emerson's biggest regret. Eight years ago, a lack of trust cost her a future with the star running back. Now an opportunity brings the nutrition entrepreneur home, where she hopes to declare a truce. But their first encounter unleashes explosive passion. Is this their second chance?

#566 SEDUCED IN SAN DIEGO
Millionaire Moguls • by Reese Ryan

There's nothing conventional about artist Jordan Jace, except his membership to the exclusive Millionaire Moguls. And when he meets marketing consultant Sasha Charles, persuading the straitlaced beauty to break some rules is an irresistible challenge. But their affair may be temporary, unless they can discover the art of love—together…

#567 ONE UNFORGETTABLE KISS
The Taylors of Temptation • by A.C. Arthur

All navy pilot Garrek Taylor ever wanted was to fly far from his family's past. But with his wings temporarily clipped, he's back in his hometown. His plans are sidetracked when he wins a date with unconventional house restorer Harper Presley. Will their combustible connection lead to an everlasting future?

#568 A BILLIONAIRE AFFAIR
Passion Grove • by Niobia Bryant

Alessandra Dalmount has been groomed to assume the joint reins of her father's empire. Now that day has arrived, forcing her to work closely with co-CEO and childhood nemesis Alek Ansah. As they battle for control of the billion-dollar conglomerate, can they turn their rivalry into an alliance of love?

Want to give in to temptation with
steamy tales of irresistible desire?

Check out **Harlequin® Presents®**,
Harlequin® Desire and
Harlequin® Kimani™ Romance books!

New books available every month!

CONNECT WITH US AT:

Harlequin.com/Community

 Facebook.com/HarlequinBooks

 Twitter.com/HarlequinBooks

 Instagram.com/HarlequinBooks

 Pinterest.com/HarlequinBooks

ReaderService.com

**ROMANCE WHEN
YOU NEED IT**

PGENRE2017